S0-FQZ-827

JEAN BELL

authorHOUSE

AuthorHouse™
1663 Liberty Drive
Bloomington, IN 47403
www.authorhouse.com
Phone: 1 (800) 839-8640

© *2017 Jean Bell. All rights reserved.*

No part of this book may be reproduced, stored in a retrieval system, or transmitted by any means without the written permission of the author.

Published by AuthorHouse 01/12/2018

ISBN: 978-1-5462-1670-4 (sc)
ISBN: 978-1-5462-1668-1 (hc)
ISBN: 978-1-5462-1669-8 (e)

Library of Congress Control Number: 2017917327

Print information available on the last page.

Any people depicted in stock imagery provided by Thinkstock are models, and such images are being used for illustrative purposes only.
Certain stock imagery © Thinkstock.

This book is printed on acid-free paper.

Because of the dynamic nature of the Internet, any web addresses or links contained in this book may have changed since publication and may no longer be valid. The views expressed in this work are solely those of the author and do not necessarily reflect the views of the publisher, and the publisher hereby disclaims any responsibility for them.

1960

The kitchen in the Strong mansion hasn't kept up with the latest trend in the Better Homes and Gardens magazine latest issue picturing carpeting in kitchens and bathrooms. Bonnie was happy about that. The ceramic hex tiles in black and white were easy for Celia, the maid, to wipe up with a mop, like the linoleum in the bakery apartment that she remembers her mother scrubbing daily on her hands and knees. The small tiles are echoed on the island counter top. White steel cabinets are reassuring in their timelessness.

Her father-in law, Mr. Strong—Bonnie only ever calls him that—has added a large window over the sink that gives a view of the backyard tennis court and swimming pool.

Ah, Bonnie thinks, *that swimming pool. It's seldom used and now in January snow is blanketing everything.* Again, it's falling in big fluffy flakes.

It's early morning. The winter sun is beginning to rise. Bonnie, shivering in her pink chenille robe, sits at the island counter with her coffee, the morning paper, and her small, shiny sharp scissors. The Strongs are often mentioned in the local section of the Copper Ridge Journal. Yes, here it is in the first column.

> January 2,1960—At the annual New Year's Strong Ball, Mr. Alfeo Strong with his wife Bonnie at his side, announced his candidacy for mayor of Copper Ridge. Bob Pilot the current mayor has opted for retirement at the end of

his term. Mr. Pilot has been mayor for the past thirty years. Mr. Strong is running unopposed.

Bonnie carefully cuts out the piece with the sharp scissors then opens the drawer beneath the island. It isn't a task she likes doing, saving clippings, but Rosalie—her mother-in law—thinks Bonnie can be relied on to save these almost daily write-ups. *Coupons*, she thinks. *Turn them in and turn back time*. She laughs aloud at this thought.

The shoe box, decorated with blue stick-on stars, and its messy, disorganized content, together with the teal green back-splash behind the counter tops, evoke memories of the waters of Lake Wakesha where Alan had died. She has returned to the lake only once— to the shore where Alan's body had been recovered. She reads the clipping again.

> August 20, 1952— The body of Alan Richard Smith, a Junior at Copper Ridge High School, was recovered, fully clothed, late yesterday afternoon from Lake Wakesha. He had been reported missing since August 15th. The county coroner ruled the death a suicide.

Four days after my wedding. Rosalie broke the news to them after she and Alfeo had left their bags in the second-floor rooms of the mansion that had been prepared for them. *In this very kitchen.* Rosalie had poured tea for the newlyweds. She gave Bonnie an envelope with her name on it. Bonnie Grace.

"The coroner gave it to me. I haven't looked inside, Bonnie."

There was a folded piece of plain white paper inside the envelope. Bonnie had trembled as she unfolded the paper. "Hocus pocus dominocus," read the script. That was all. Bonnie had frozen in disbelief. She couldn't speak. A deep, dark numbness had overcome her. Alfeo had made a scretchy noise, like a trapped rabbit or turtle. *Did they make sounds?*

Bonnie puts the now yellowed clipping back in the shoebox. She wishes she hadn't thrown the note away. She rifles through more clippings.

> June 22, 1956—Twin daughters, Lucy Ann, and Loretta Ann, were born to Mr. and Mrs. Thomas Jones of 113 D Street. Mr. Jones served two years in the United States Army during the Korean war and his wife, Joanne, was named Girl Scout of the Year for her work as troop leader in the Kits for Korea effort during that same period.

Joanne—twins, of course. Tom is so proud. He works hard at his landscaping and snow removal business. One time, at a party, Joanne had taken Bonnie aside and said quietly, "I know why Alan killed himself, humm."

"I don't want to talk about it, Joanne. You didn't know my brother at all."

Why had she brought this up—after four years? Still that silly sing-song, humm.

"I'm pregnant, Joanne," Bonnie, flustered, had cut Joanne off from continuing her know-it all gossip. The wound is still open, thrumming beneath the apparent glittery surface of her now wealthy lifestyle.

It has been a struggle. Bonnie has to beg Alfeo for sex. It's always an impersonal encounter. "Do you really love me, Alfeo?" she's asked more than once. And always the same perfunctory answer.

"Of course, Bonnie. I'm here, aren't I?"

Bonnie had wanted to name their son, Van. After Van Johnson, her favorite movie actor, but Alfeo insisted on Alan. Bonnie never looks at their son without experiencing a remorseful feeling. She is glad that Rosalie takes charge of the child. He looks more like Mr. Strong than herself or Alfeo. *Funny.*

And Alfeo isn't often at the big house on C street. He's with his father, away for weeks at a time in Minnesota. Another clipping is in her hand.

> June 21, 1955—Mr. Earl V. Strong has taken over a foundry in Hibbing, Minnesota, located in the Mesabi range, where a new deposit of iron ore has been found. Mr. Strong owns three other foundries in the Copper Ridge area.

Maybe now, as mayor, Alfeo would have to be around, available for the town folks' grumbles.

Some small, but rewarding things have changed since Bonnie's move to the castle. Her mother and father now live in a comfortable house on Caspian Street, near the Nanninis. Rosalie— having finally decided to drive—often spends time with Bonnie's mother, co-hosting the regular meeting of the Holy Martyrs Altar Society. Daddy has a garden and had once won a blue ribbon at the Marquette County fair for his Ruby Cresent fingerling potatoes. Gus is in the air force. He had enlisted at the tail end of the Korean war. Annie lives in Green Bay, with her seven-year-old son, George Alan, and her husband, Carl Belin, manager of the Arthur Murray Ballroom Dance Studio.

The City Bakery—with its twenty-six steps to Alan and Mama and Daddy—is no more.

> December 12, 1955— A massive fire yesterday destroyed the City Bakery building on Margaret Street during an ongoing record snowfall. The fire trucks were unable to reach the fire on time, due to the high snow drifts. The bakery owner, Tolly Gregory, said that one of the large ovens had overheated due to a faulty thermostat. The Bruno house next door was also badly damaged. Mr. and Mrs. Bruno were away at the time. Mrs. Bruno's father, Mr. Stephano Rizzardi, 89, alone in the house, was overcome by smoke and did not survive.

That same year, in another clipping, Bishop Elmer announced the decision of the Marquette chancery office to close the convent at Holy Martyrs Church in Copper Ridge. Bonnie seldom thinks of Sister Carol and her prophetic prediction that Bonnie would "never be happy as a married woman." Bonnie sighs. She hopes Sister Carol is happy at the mission in Australia.

As Bonnie randomly begins to pull out other fragile clippings from the shoe box—some of the edges torn—a flood of memories continues to wash over her. Bonnie, president of the Copper Ridge Treble Clef Music Club— though she hasn't played the piano since Alan's death.

Golf partners with Rosalie on Tuesday Ladies Day. One year they had won the UP ladies golf championship held at the Maple Grove Country Club in Iron Range. Rosalie was first, of course, but Bonnie was a close second. Bonnie stuffs today's article from the Copper Ridge Journal into the shoe box. *What was important has now become small pieces of newsprint,* she thinks.

Not one mention of the sacrifices Bonnie required of others in order to reach her goal. They were empty of Alan—her brother. He had been a sacrifice, as had her still grieving parents, and Rosalie—bereft of Jean—and herself, constantly pushing back against Alan's persistent shadow. And Alfeo. Never talked about, but Bonnie knows Alan and Alfeo had loved one another.

Bonnie slowly covers the box and puts it back in the drawer. Mrs. Prianti would be coming early this morning to help with the tea sandwiches for Rosalie's afternoon bridge club.

The snow is falling more rapidly now, completely covering two chairs that had been left out near the pool. They look like stumpy sheeted ghosts. *Rosalie will be getting up soon—and the boy.*

The weather promises to turn colder. Bonnie likes the cold. Cold is her friend.

Marquette, Michigan 1932-1937

Chapter 1

They said she was born at home, not a fancy place, in an area called Trowbridge Park, in a two-story log cabin. It was winter. As an adult, she listened to stories of things that happened, or wondered at the few pictures hanging on walls, or lying in drawers, or in albums, whose pages had no arrangement of time or place.

From hushed conversations between her parents—as well as from those aunts and uncles who still attended family funerals—she glimpsed small peeks into her family's past, what they were like before her birth. Some things she remembered. The time during the Great Depression, was always a source of curiosity for her, and she pieced memories together in her mind as best she could.

Bonnie's mama, Helen, was young—barely twenty—when she gave birth. A grainy picture showed her with Baby Bonnie, Mama looking a little scared and the baby clutching at Mama's engagement necklace, an amber stone embedded in silver filigree on a thin silver chain. "This kid likes pretty things," her daddy was believed to have said. Bonnie's daddy was ten years older than Mama. Their engagement photo, always displayed on their bedroom dresser, showed a sweet-faced girl with dark wavy hair, cut short in a 1920's flapper style, her eyes glancing to the right, as if she were looking at something odd. The man had sleeked back black hair, a trim mustache, and kind eyes, that some called bedroom eyes. People found him "Clark Gable" handsome.

One of her dad's sisters, Aunt Lillian, had said, "Before he met Mama, he was engaged to a girl who broke things off. That girl broke his heart."

Will, that was her daddy's name, was a musician. Another picture showed him in a banjo band taken during the twenties, wearing a straw boater and a stripped jacket. Everyone in the band was dressed the same. They were seated in one row, on a stage, before a closed curtain, holding their instruments neck up on their laps, all facing forward and unsmiling. Maybe it was taken in a dance hall. Maybe it was on a stage before a silent picture show. No one seemed to know.

Aunt Lillian said, "Your mother looked a lot like the girl who had broken Daddy's heart. He was crazy about her, bought her a ring and everything."

Her mom, Helen, was seventeen when she attended a dance where Will was playing in the band. He had spotted Mama on the dance floor, and he stepped down from the bandstand to ask her to dance. That was in the summer of 1930. Mama always said Daddy was a terrible dancer.

"He just shuffles back and forth in a sort of one-step," Mama had once complained to Aunt Lillian.

In any case, they were married just six months later, before a priest, in February, at 5:00 o'clock in the morning. It was a quiet affair, almost an elopement. There was no Mass, because there was no money, though the banns had been read unbeknownst to Helen's parents. Will's brother, Francis, and another of his sisters, Tilly, were witnesses.

Helen's mother, Grandmother Hilda Johnson, was opposed to the union because Will was a Catholic, and she was a staunch Swedish Methodist. She carried on and on when the two were courting. She offered Helen a fur coat and a car not to marry Will, but to no avail. Helen was supposed to go to nursing school. She had the nurse's watch and everything. She had to wait a year; she was only seventeen, having skipped a grade because she was so smart.

The quick, secret ceremony took place anyway, and when Grandma Johnson found out, Helen was cut off. That was that. She had converted to Catholicism to marry Daddy, promising to raise any offspring in the faith. The conversion didn't take however, as she failed attend church for years and years, returning only when one of her sons committed suicide.

On the morning of Helen's wedding it began to snow in blinding wet flakes. Mama often said she thought about calling off the wedding because she wasn't sure the wedding party could get to the cathedral for the ceremony.

Seemed it was always snowing in Michigan's Upper Peninsula. Sometimes the snow was so deep that Daddy had to pull a sled to the store to get groceries. All that white. So heavy. Blowing about, like the world was in a snow globe, being shaken up by some unseen hand. The sky blanketed the ground with smothering flakes. No one minded the snow. It was a way of life. Even the old people could be seen outside their doors, shoveling a path, and calling out to one another, "Another big one, eh?"

Well, of course, everyone made it to the church, and the vows were spoken in record time, in the early morning dark, in the downtown cathedral.

Helen and Will lived for a time, at first, with Will's Ma and Pa in Marquette. His mom, Marie, was French Canadian and spoke mostly English, but sometimes French. No one knew Grandpa Smith's origin. Uncle Francis said he was adopted by a family in Michigan by the name of Smith. Adoption records were closed at that time, so his true family background remained a mystery. Grandma Marie met Grandpa Ollie at a dance, too. She was playing the piano with a band at a local bar. That's where he first saw her. He went everywhere she was playing, and finally got up the courage to ask her to meet him in a park on a Sunday afternoon for ice cream. It was all so romantic.

Chapter 2

Summers in the Upper Peninsula were short. People spent most of their times outside in gardens, or picking wild berries, or trapping rabbits for stew. Beer drinking went on year-round. A lot of beer drinking. Daddy's father, Grandpa Smith, drank his beer from a white grandfather mug. Children liked to climb onto his lap, knowing they would be rewarded with a sip of the fizzy stuff. One picture of Grandpa Smith, in a sepia tinted wedding portrait, revealed that he was quite handsome as a young man. His wife, Marie, looked beautiful and soft by his side.

One picture of Mama showed her with a slightly crooked jaw. Aunt Tilly said Mama was a lot of fun. She loved to dance and followed Will to the bars wherever he had a gig. Tilly said one night there was a fight over Mama outside a bar, between two men who were drunkenly arguing over who would get to dance with her. One of the guys threw a punch, missing his opponent and popping Mama instead.

Her jaw was wired shut for six of the nine months she was pregnant with Bonnie, the first grandchild born into the Smith clan. It was an easy birth. Bonnie was just a few ounces shy of seven pounds. She was born in the upstairs bedroom at 3:33 AM on a February morning. Will sent a neighbor for the midwife a little after midnight when Mama's contractions had started at regular intervals. Bonnie cried right away, even before her bottom was spanked.

After the birth of their grandchild, Helen and her parents reconciled. Another picture shows Bonnie being held by her mother's father, Grandpa Johnson. The baby is wearing a tight satin bonnet.

Grandma Johnson believed this would correct a noticeable protruding of Bonnie's left ear. It failed to correct the outcropping, even though Bonnie wore the bonnet for two years, night and day. Her grandmother finally conceded defeat saying, "This child must never wear her hair pulled back."

Chapter 3

Bonnie's mama had a lot of girlfriends with babies of their own. They walked together, pushing their black baby prams along the main street during the summer. Mama told her later that every time they strolled past the J, C. Penny store, Bonnie would cry non-stop. The girls thought that was funny. As a grown woman, Bonnie still enters the Penny store with some trepidation and a general feeling of uncertainty, then she laughs for being such a ninny. *It's nothing*, she thinks to herself.

When Bonnie was about three years old, her parents moved from Marquette to Houghton, Michigan for a brief time because of her daddy's job on a cruise boat that went around the five Great Lakes. The girls stayed in the upper apartment of a brick building while Daddy was away, playing trumpet with the ship's dance band.

Bonnie's memory of that time is hazy, but she recalls the Apple Lady, who lived in the downstairs apartment. Maybe it was a grocery store. She wore an apron with two pockets stitched on that looked like red apples with green leaves attached. She kept candy in one pocket, and sometimes gave Bonnie a piece. Bonnie would reach up and hug the Apple Lady's skirt, grabbing at the pocket to receive her reward.

Bonnie also recalls the steep hills, steeper than those in Marquette. She and Mama didn't go outside a lot in Houghton, even though there was no snow. The cruise boats only ran in the summer. In a family photo album, there is a picture of the boat Daddy was on, clipped from an old yellowed newspaper. It was called *The South American.*

The stay in Houghton only lasted one summer. Soon they were back in Marquette, in a shack house, in a place called the Picqua location.

That's where her daddy worked then. People said he was lucky to have a job at the Piqua Woodworking Plant, as so many men were out of work. The house was small and squareish, with no front porch, or steps. The front door was never used, because of the long drop. The usable entrance was through a back-screen door that led directly into the tiny kitchen. The kitchen floor was packed black dirt. There was no bathroom. Bonnie had to pee in a bucket and Mama and Daddy peed in a little house in the back.

An old picture shows another person with them now. Annie. Someone they called Bonnie's sister. Annie is about two years old in this picture, pretty and shy, her head tilted to one side, blonde curls all over her head. She is standing beside Bonnie. They are holding hands. Bonnie, at almost four, is a lot taller. Annie is wearing some sort of diaper, hanging loosely from beneath her skirt. The dresses are nondescript and ill-fitting.

The sisters shared a bedroom with no windows. Bonnie always remembered a dream—a nightmare really—where she saw a team of horses pulling some sort of wheel-less wagon, making horrible clanking noises, coming toward her, and she couldn't scream or stop them. There was smoke coming from the horses' nostrils. She was terrified. No one came to rescue her from the huge beasts. From that time on her fear of animals grew.

There are no pictures of the shack, but Bonnie remembers that in this house there were bed bugs. In the mornings, she and Annie cried, their small bodies covered with ugly red bites. Mama cried too. "Please, Will, you've got to do something."

Daddy got busy, securing each window with tape—maybe there was only one, maybe two—and the unused front door, and the back door with the torn screen off the small kitchen. He held up two canisters, one in each hand, and yelled, "Everyone out!" Bonnie, her mother, and Annie stood in front of the house in the scraggly front yard, holding hands as Daddy called out, "Deadly poison canisters," and released the gas. He wore a blue checkered bandana over his face and his eyes were barely visible. Mama, Bonnie, and Annie screamed as he leaped from the stairless front door, pulling it tight as he jumped. "Oh, Will, I was so scared" said Mama.

Daddy can do anything, Bonnie thought at that time. She adored him. He could get rid of bugs. She despised bugs, especially spiders. She liked to trap the daddy-long-leg spiders and pull off their legs, one at a time, so they couldn't move, then she would squish their remaining round, brownish bodies.

They spent the next few days with Grandma and Grandpa Smith. When the bedbugs had been vanquished and the poison gas had blown out the one window, they returned to the Piqua house. Mama was gone for several days after that, and Daddy became the cook. Bonnie loved his tomato soup and hamburger concoction that he dumped over saltine crackers in a cereal bowl. "Why can't Mama make that?" she had asked. Daddy said it was his special recipe, and that's all he knew how to make.

Mama returned with a new baby called August William, Augie for short. August was Daddy's middle name. Bonnie said his name over and over in a sing-song way. "August William Smith, August William Smith." She liked to sing. She sang her sister's name in the same manner, "Annie Marie Smith, Annie Marie Smith," and her own name, "Bonnie Grace Smith, Bonnie Grace Smith." These names were imprinted on her heart.

Chapter 4

When Bonnie was five, she overheard Mama and Daddy talking about sending her to kindergarten. *What is kindergarten?* she wondered.

"We live too far from the school for her to walk, so we'll have to keep her home this year," Mama said.

She sat on her mother's lap at times, being read to from picture books. Once, while looking with Mama at a picture of a brightly colored fairy tale house set in a wood, the page seemed to swim before her eyes, and she started to read the words written there. After that she read words everywhere, especially on signs and cereal boxes.

Chapter 5

Annie got sick and she was taken to the Pest House where kids had to go who had catchy, dangerous diseases. "Scarlet Fever," the county nurse said. A man came and tacked a quarantine sign on the front door with no steps, so no one would come into the house. No one ever came anyway.

Daddy took the family to visit Annie at the Pest House, but they could only see her from a distance while sitting in their car. A lady in a tall wooden rocking chair was on the porch, holding Annie. Bonnie could tell it was Annie because her small blond head was visible above the swaddling blanket. When Annie saw Daddy's car she waved, and the lady in the rocking chair waved along with her.

There was no grass around the Pest House, only sand. Mama and Daddy waved back and called her name from the car window of Daddy's Model T Ford. One time it was raining so hard—with thunder and lightning—that Bonnie became frightened and cried because she thought the car was going to sink into the muddy ground. There was no calming her, and she was always terrified of thunderstorms after that.

Chapter 6

Now Bonnie was six years old, and the law said she had to attend school for the first grade. The family moved to another place in Marquette, this one with an upstairs apartment like the one in Houghton. There was a front balcony on that house, painted white with a wooden railing. It had a real flushing toilet. It was close to the Catholic Cathedral School, so Bonnie could walk there and back.

Her family went to the Holy Name Cathedral Church every Sunday and Holy day for Mass. Not Mama, though; Daddy told everyone to always pray for Mama because the conversion hadn't taken.

The church was cold and gloomy, even with the tall stained-glass windows and endless center aisle. Bonnie was curious about the goings on about her and spent a good deal of the time turning around on the hard pews to look at the people who were filtering into their seats, bending on one knee first, before getting into the pew. She wondered why they had to do this. Daddy did it, too. He had Bonnie practice at home, but she wasn't ever sure which knee to start with.

The women all wore hats or black lacy veils on their heads. Bonnie wore a hat, too, a bonnet of straw that had a thin elastic attached to the sides that looped under her chin. The elastic hurt, but the hat had to stay on. One time, as she was looking back at the people coming in, a nun, or sister, as they were called—raised her arm and pointed with her finger toward the altar. The black habit and piercing eyes terrified Bonnie, causing her to feel guilt for the first time. She quickly looked ahead and remained unmoving for the next hour. The nun sat right in the pew behind them. Bonnie felt embarrassed and humiliated, and hoped her daddy hadn't noticed. The church-going never became a welcome excursion, but the trip had to be made every Sunday or bad things would happen.

School was confusing, too. Everyone had their own books—not with words, just individual letters. 'C' pictured with a cat, 'T' with a toy top; 'A' with some sort of mark over it. They were made to say "*cuh-ah-tuh*." Never "cat." She did her best with this new language and managed to get a passing grade on her report card. Her mama told her it was the language of phonics, and that it would disappear when she passed into second grade.

"Is that like the language they say in church? Will that vanish, too?"

"No, Bonnie, that's called Latin," she said. That will never change. It's a dead language, but it's not buried," she answered with a little smile.

"Why don't you come to church with us, Mama?" Bonnie finally got up the courage to ask her mother that day. So many questions had been jumbling in her mind. Other mothers went to church. Why not her own? Would bad things happen to her mother? Why didn't the conversion take?

"I'm not comfortable with the way they do things, Bonnie. Maybe someday I'll go. God is taking his time with me. It's my own personal problem. Don't worry about it, honey."

Mama knows so much, Bonnie thought. Her Aunt Tillie told Bonnie that Mama knew a lot because she had skipped a grade. More than one person had said that about Mama. Even Mama herself brought it up from time to time. She'd had to wait a year to leave for college, so Bonnie knew that story was true. Lucky for Daddy, she changed her mind about going after that year had passed.

Chapter 7

One day, Daddy said they were going to visit Grandma Johnson in the next town. It was twenty miles away. That was where Mama had grown up. The town was called Nauganee. Bonnie thought that was a strange name. Mama said it was an Indian name. Mama sat in the passenger seat and Bonnie, Annie, and Augie sat in the back with Bonnie and Annie on the seat and Augie on a little wooden stool on the floor. The road was winding and tall trees were on each side like watchtowers.

Sometimes there were hills and Daddy would call out, "Hold on, we're going down," and we would all laugh. Not Mama though. She didn't drive. She said she had started to learn, but once, while turning into the driveway of her house she had stepped on the gas pedal instead of the brake and had driven through the garage door. She said she got out of the car crying and vowed never to try driving again. Grandpa Johnson had agreed with that.

She was a great assistant driver, though, always telling Daddy to slow down in a loud voice.

"Will, slow down, watch where you're going!" She would firmly grip the car door handle, her foot pressed into the front floor board as if she had the power to stop a certain catastrophe.

Grandma Johnson's house was different from Grandma Smith's. Proper somehow. All of the houses on that street were the same on both sides. Each house had a lawn in front. Not like the sandy, scrubby stuff at the Smith house. Grandpa Johnson always kept the grass so close with his hand mower. There was an enclosed front porch with curtained windows on two sides. Mama said that Grandma sat there most days in her rocking chair with a crochet needle and a spool of thick cotton in her hands, keeping her one eye on the neighbors by slightly lifting the edge of a curtain.

"There goes that Bergstrom boy. He's trouble," she'd say expelling a hmph through her nose, or, "I see the Lindstroms have company. Wonder who their visitors are this time." Another hmph. Her comments were mostly addressed to herself, under her breath. She spoke them aloud if anyone happened to be near. She was a great commentator on the neighborhood doings.

Sometimes she said, "Look, the house across the street. Someone's peeking at our house. It's that Mrs. Bergstrom. She's so nosy."

Just off her porch was the living room furnished with a piano and a sofa. The sofa was scratchy, "horsehair" Mama explained, "that would never wear out." No one sat on it, though Bonnie did try it out. No one played the piano. The best part of the living room was the stand in one corner with a radio on it. Grandma had a chair before it where she liked to sit and listen to a show called "The Breakfast Club." Grandpa liked to listen to the fights. He always talked about Joe Louis. "The Brown Bomber," he called him.

Spaces were important to Bonnie. She was afraid of so many things. She had to memorize every new environment, to figure out where to hide, where she could be safe. In Grandma and Grandpa Johnson's house, she had immediately begun to make her mental map. Upstairs was a long bathroom. The bathtub was against the side of the outside wall and stood on curved feet. The toilet and sink were also lined up in this manner, on the same side. There was one small window which Bonnie's mother opened and leaned out as she smoked her cigarettes. Grandma didn't know that Mama smoked. Grandpa Johnson smoked, too, outside though, and he chewed tobacco and made loud gargly noises in his throat just before spitting out an ugly brown wad into the garden dirt.

The closet in the upstairs hall was filled with sewing stuff like torn rags which Grandma used to make braided rugs, button boxes, needle cases, and other things that Bonnie found curious. Grandma once showed Bonnie how to sew a button onto a square of cotton cloth. It was a large button, black, with two holes in it, and Bonnie pricked her finger several times while going about this task. She saw her blood seep out. She wasn't sure she liked sewing, and she knew she hated the sight of blood. Bonnie thought she could squeeze into the sewing closet if she needed to hide; thunder storms were unpredictable.

Behind the living room was a dining room, with a table covered in a lace tablecloth, a hutch displaying pretty cups and glasses, and a side board with drawers. The kids were not allowed to touch any of these things. They all sat at a rectangular table in the kitchen. Grandma passed out tarts and saffron bread made the day before. She served the kids homebrewed root beer from Grandpa's cellar. The adults had coffee, pouring out the liquid from their cups, then sipping the cooled drink from the saucer.

Daddy told the kids to say thank you for the tarts, but Annie wouldn't. Daddy kept yelling at her to say it, but Annie just stood there. Daddy gave her the worst spanking, holding her aloft by one small arm while he whacked her bottom.

Mama cried, "Will stop!" Finally, he did, looking red-faced and ashamed. Annie was just four years old. Bonnie was terribly frightened. She had never seen her daddy be mean. Augie, so small and scared, ran into another room. Things became quiet around the kitchen after that, and Grandma kept giving Mama an *I told you so look.*

Grandpa Johnson was out in his garden. He had a big garden in the back yard, where he spent most of his day during the summer months. He often took Bonnie there, and they pulled green onions together, then he cleaned and chopped the onions into small circles, even the green tops. He made onion sandwiches, arranging the circles on buttered rye bread. Bonnie declined to taste the sandwich, because she had never had an uncooked onion, but Grandpa said it was good, so she finally took a small bite. It was sharp on her tongue and made her eyes water, but she decided she liked it. Grandpa had fixed it, after all.

Grandpa was bald, and he usually wore a cap. He took off his cap as they were all leaving for Marquette and asked Bonnie to kiss his bald head, right in front of everyone. She did as he asked. Grandpa bent down so she could reach to top of his head. He smiled expectantly at her. Everyone standing there was grinning, too. She planted a kiss on his warm head. It was fuzzy and sweaty. Bonnie felt embarrassed because people started to laugh. She hadn't like doing it, but thought it was expected of her, and she didn't want Daddy to spank her, too.

At some point, there was an unspoken sense that Annie was Grandma Johnson's favorite and Bonnie belonged to Grandpa. Maybe it was because Annie had been spanked and Bonnie had given the kiss.

Bonnie remembered two other rooms upstairs, a bedroom for Grandma and one for Grandpa. Bonnie thought that was strange.

"Why don't they sleep in the same bedroom?" she asked her mother as they were driving back to Marquette.

"They just don't," was all her mother said.

Grandma Smith's house was more fun. Daddy's brothers and sisters lived there, and they seemed to do as they pleased. They had a piano, too, which her Aunt Lillian played. In that house, everyone was always playing and singing music. Grandma Smith loved to talk about her early band days. Now she just liked to play poker, staying up into the small hours with Grandpa Smith and some people Bonnie didn't know. They laughed a lot and told jokes, and drank beer and smoked cigarettes in ivory holders, and snacked from a tray of crackers and liverwurst.

Daddy's youngest brother, Pauly, had red hair and freckles. Bonnie, Annie, and Augie tried to avoid him, as he always gave them a pinch or smack if he could manage it. No one stopped him either. "That's just Pauly," Grandpa Smith said. "He's hard to control."

Aunt Lillian told the story about Uncle Pauly running away from home when he was sixteen because he hated school. No one heard from him until many years later, when he turned up drunk, telling his mother he had been all over the world serving in the Merchant Marines.

Well, he had tried the U.S. Navy, too, he said, but had been kicked out—dishonorably discharged—then he was accepted into the Merchant Marines. He shoveled coal into huge boilers below the ship's deck, and played poker during his down time. He brought his mother an embossed roll of silk from India. He laughed as he tried to show her how to tie it in a sari. She laughed, too, as he twisted the cloth around and around her. Grandma was just happy that he had come home.

Mama's brother, Uncle Lemmy, was a drunk, too. Mama said they had taken Bonnie as a new baby, all the way from Marquette to Hibbing, Minnesota in Daddy's Ford Model T. That's where Lemmy had called from, having fallen asleep drunk one night in a railroad box car in Negaunee, not realizing the train would start going, finally waking up the next morning in Hibbing. Later in life, he married Aunt Violet, and Grandma Johnson had to dis-own him, too, because Violet was an Italian.

Chapter 8

Several men came outside of Grandma Smith's house one day when Bonnie's was there with her mother and brother and sister. They were musician friends of Daddy's and they stood outside laughing The men were loud, and they were smashing the tops off beer bottles on rocks. Bonnie peeked at them through the small kitchen window as they staggered nearer to the back door.

"Bonnie, come away from the window," whispered Mama as she pulled the children close to her. "Come into the front hall where there's no window."

"Hey, Helen, open the door; we need a bottle opener," they called to Mama.

"We'll be okay," Mama said quietly, "Don't cry or they'll know we're here." She took silver knives and pushed them into the door jambs, so they couldn't get in. There were no keys for the doors. Bonnie and Annie were so afraid, trying not to make noise, biting their lips, hanging on to Mama's skirt while she secured the doors. They couldn't help crying. Augie was asleep upstairs.

Finally, Daddy showed up and said something to the drunken men, and they took off still laughing and singing. Will took Mama and the kids back to their balcony house near the Cathedral School. He seemed to be upset with Mama, and she was crying by then, too.

"Helen, you've got to stop flirting with these guys in the bar," he yelled at her. "They get the wrong idea. You know that. What's wrong with you? I'm playing these gigs to earn money for the family. Maybe you should stay home."

"Will, I like to dance, that's all. I'm not flirting." She said through her tears.

"Humph," was all he said. They didn't talk much for several days after that.

Chapter 9

When Bonnie turned seven, she and Annie went alone together for a train ride. They were to spend the summer with Grandma and Grandpa Johnson. Daddy had lost his job when the Piqua plant closed, and Mama was expecting again. The family had to move back in with Grandma and Grandpa Smith while Daddy looked for work. Grandma Johnson said she would take the two girls, but not Augie. There wasn't room, and two was all she could handle for a whole summer.

The girls were so excited, waiting at the train station. The train arrived, seeming too fierce shooting white smoke from the engine smoke stack. Daddy helped the girls onto the train, cautioning them not to talk to anyone but the conductor. He walked into the train car with them and saw them to their empty seats. He handed Bonnie two important looking tickets with Nauganee stamped onto the front.

"Here you go, girls," he said. "Be sure and behave for your grandparents. They're doing your mama and me a big favor."

The train had green velvet seats with high backs, and the girls held hands for the whole twenty miles to the downtown Negaunee station. Bonnie felt apprehensive and exhilarated at the same time. The rocking train made Annie sick to her stomach and she had to throw up.

Bonnie took off her blue beanie cap and caught the vomit in it. She left the hat as far under the seat as she could get it, horrified. She feared being arrested if anyone noticed. It did smell, if you were sitting close by, but the clouds of cigarette smoke drifting from the other passengers helped disguise the pungent odor.

Grandma Johnson met them at the depot. "Where's your hat, Bonnie?" she asked, after giving them a hug.

"I'm sorry Grandma." Bonnie said. "I left it on the train. I hope you're not mad at me." Annie looked gratefully at her sister.

"I'll just have to crochet you another one, white this time, so it'll be easier to see," she said.

"You should keep your hat on in public places, you know. Doesn't your mother teach you manners?"

Still holding hands, Bonnie and Annie walked with Grandma up a big hill, past a lake, that Grandma said was dead and not for swimming. The lake shimmered with a mysterious light, which people could see even brighter at night. It smelled, too. Grandpa Johnson said it was from sulfur that leaked in from the copper mines. "They don't mine copper here anymore. It's all iron ore now." Grandpa was a retired mine guard, and he knew all about such things.

Grandpa belonged to a lodge, the Moose Lodge. Grandma didn't like the lodge. She said all they did was drink and curse. Grandma and Grandpa hardly ever said anything to each other. "We've been married too long." she said. "There's no need to say anything. I know what he wants—his big breakfast of potatoes and eggs, and rye bread ham sandwiches with butter. He won't eat that fake stuff. I have to buy cream from a local farmer and make real butter. He's a lot of work, eh."

Grandpa showed them how to open the backyard fence gate and walked them down the short rocky path behind the house, where he picked up a few flat stones and flung them into the dead water, where they bounced in a defiant way, splashing up little sprays, bringing the lake back to life. He showed them how to do it, and sometimes it worked. They laughed in triumph when the stones skipped over the top of the water.

"Grandma, who are those people across the lake who are always waving their hands about?" Annie asked.

"Those are the dummies," Grandma explained. "They can't hear or speak. When they meet people, they put their hands over their ears and their mouths, like this." She gestured with both hands. "Then people will understand that they're deaf and dumb. Sometimes they wear a sign hanging around their neck, telling people this. That's when they come to the door trying to sell pencils. I never buy anything from them." She gave a big sigh.

This intrigued Bonnie, and she sometimes made up a game where she couldn't hear or speak when she was being teased. The teasing occurred mostly about her attire. Grandma Johnson made all their dresses from empty flour sacks. The sacks had small, colorful patterns of tiny flowers and Bonnie thought them pretty, but the fabric was scratchy on her skin. Poor people bought them at the seed mill for just ten cents a bag. The bags also made good dish towels and wash cloths in Grandma's capable hands.

The boys in Marquette where Mama and Daddy lived were the biggest teasers. "Wearing a flour sack, are you, Bonnie?" they called. "Bonnie Sack, Bonnie Sack, give us a smack." Bonnie knew they meant kiss, not smack. They were just dumb boys.

The teasing didn't usually bother Bonnie because she felt in her bones that she was pretty, even dressed in a sack. The neighbors near the Johnsons often remarked that she looked just like her mother, and Bonnie thought her mama was beautiful. Her sister, Annie, was even prettier, with her soft, blonde, curly hair, and big blue eyes. Bonnie wanted to be as pretty as her sister. *If I had pretty things, I'd be the one everyone thinks is the most beautiful*, she thought.

Bonnie, being taller, was able to lord it over her sister. Annie didn't kowtow, though. When Bonnie got too bossy, Annie had a frustrating way of quitting a game of hopscotch or jacks when Bonnie was ahead, thus preventing her from declaring victory. This infuriated Bonnie, but there was nothing she could do about it short of calling Annie a poor loser. Annie would just laugh and walk away.

Annie kept close to Grandma Johnson for much of the summer. Bonnie spent her time in the garden with Grandpa. He showed her which plants were the good ones and which were weeds. He let her pull weeds and gave her the task of weeding from the flowers planted around the side of the house. Sometimes Bonnie wasn't sure which was which because the plants were so small. Still she pulled them, even if they were the wrong ones. It made her feel guilty, so she never told anyone.

Every week day she traveled with Grandpa along a grassy path, up the hill across the street, to a small shack with a fenced in area at the top, where he kept two pigs. "They're next winter's bacon," he laughed. He said the shack was called a hen house, but there were no hens, only geese. The geese were mean, always chasing Bonnie, and she was afraid of them.

After feeding the pigs, Grandpa would take her up another hill, this time along a sidewalk, to Richard's Ice Cream Store. Richard was Grandpa's first name, but it wasn't his ice cream store. It belonged to a different Richard. Bonnie felt privileged for there was never ice cream at the Smiths. She always ordered "Chocolate, please, one scoop," and made it last until they were back at the house. Chocolate turned out to be her favorite. She ate it all except for the empty cone which she offered to Annie, who looked hurt.

"Can't I go with you and Grandpa to the ice cream store?" she cried.

"You have to stay with Grandma, Annie, you're too small to help Grandpa with the pigs."

"I'm afraid of the pigs, Bonnie."

"Maybe next year when you grow taller. Grandma doesn't want you to be hurt. You're Grandma's girl. I'm Grandpa's girl."

"Grandma never goes out, Bonnie. She just likes to peek out the porch window."

Bonnie felt a little bad but liked the feeling of being the chosen one for the ice cream.

On Saturdays Bonnie and Grandpa took excursions to a cemetery on another hill. Grandpa trimmed grass around certain headstones. He told Bonnie these were her uncles, aunts, and some cousins who had passed on a long time ago. They all had names on the stones ending in son or datter. He said that's how people knew who they belonged to, like he was the son of John, so his name was Johnson.

Little musings circled in Bonnie's head as she thought about this. It was another language that seemed to be dead like Latin. Perhaps because everyone in the ground was dead, but Grandpa wasn't, but someday he would be dead, because he was so old and his hair was gone. Was his son, Lemmy, called Lemmy Richardson, or Lemmy *Richardjohnson,* or what? She didn't ask. She wondered if Grandpa would go to heaven, not being Catholic.

Grandpa had put up a swing in the garage for Bonnie and Annie. He had to open the garage door so they could use it, otherwise their feet would hit against it if they swung too high. The swing had ropes made of raw hemp, and the rope would dig into their hands, like the horsehair couch dug into their legs, but still they had fun with the swing, never having had one of their own.

"We have to remember to open the garage door when we swing, Annie," Bonnie said importantly. Remember Mama said she drove through it once with a car. Our legs could to right through it because we like to swing high."

"My turn to swing, Bonnie. You need to push me so I can get started."

"Girls, time to come in now for lunch," called Grandma. She was always calling them in for something. Grandma never let them stay in the yard for long.

The kitchen in Grandma Johnson's house had a big iron stove with four lids on top and an oven beneath. Grandma had to pull out a drawer under the oven to stir the wood burning beneath it. There was a pile of kindling alongside the stove in a metal box. "It's such a job, getting this stove going every morning," she said. "Grandpa never helps."

Grandpa kept a pile of wood stacked along the garage wall. He said a certain size of pile was called a cord, and he liked to keep three or four cords ready for Grandma's stove and for heating the house during the winter. Grandma was always busy putting good things into the baking oven. There was even a warming oven above the burners. It all seemed complicated to Bonnie. Grandma Smith's stove was a lot smaller and seemed to work in some other way, she wasn't sure how.

Off the kitchen was a small room called the pantry. It had an ice box, kept cold by a large block of ice. A truck came every week and the driver put in a new block of ice. The ice was heavy, and he carried it with big tongs over his shoulder, like a sack of potatoes. Grandma emptied a pan every day under the icebox; it was filled with water from the melting ice. Bonnie and Annie liked to chase the truck as it was leaving so that they could pick up the chips of ice that fell from the back of the truck bed. The chips were cold on their tongues and some of them were a little sharp edged and sawdusty. No matter, it was fun, a treat of sorts.

The pantry shelves reached to the ceiling. On the shelves were everyday dishes and cooking pots, and stacks of napkins and table cloths. One shelf was just for sugar cookies, saffron breads, buns, and tarts which Grandma was always baking. She showed the girls how to knead dough when she was making bread. That was hard work. They had to keep pushing and turning the dough with the heels of their hands for a long time, waiting for Grandma to say, "Now it's ready." She said it like this— "Now it is *red*," with her voice down low, and *dee*, with a lilt up on the last syllable. Mama said she had a Swedish accent, because she had been raised in Sweden until she was fifteen.

Grandma's arms looked soft and doughy to Bonnie. Grandma said she was glad of the help with the kneading as this work was hard on her heart. "My heart's not too good," she said.

Bonnie worried about this. *Would her Grandma die while they were visiting? What did Grandma's heart look like? How did it get not good? What would Grandpa do?* She worked harder and harder at the kneading, hoping to stave off the uncertainty. She yearned to go back to Marquette where she felt safe.

On part of one shelf in the pantry were the knives, forks, and spoons, each separated and standing in their own tall glass. There was a big tray with larger utensils organized in separate compartments. The pantry smelled delicious and was Bonnie's favorite part of the house.

Just off the kitchen was another door leading to the cellar. The cellar had a damp, musty, unpleasant smell. When she was asked, Bonnie went carefully down the narrow wooden steps toward the one light at the bottom. There another door stood on the left, leading to more shelves filled with jars and jars of peaches, pears, cherries, pickles, and something called chow-chow.

Bonnie had never seen so much food. She would select the desired jar and head back up the stairs. On her way, to the left, she saw the bottles of root beer that Grandpa brewed, standing in a side cupboard. *So much good stuff in such an unpleasant place*, she thought.

A tall board fence separated their house from the house to the west which belonged to Grandma's sister, Aunt Lyda and her husband Uncle Oscar Edmondson. The sisters visited daily over the fence, talking in Swedish, just the tops of their heads visible to one another.

Once Aunt Lyda invited Bonnie and Annie and Grandma over for lunch. The girls put on their newest flour-sack dresses. Grandma wore a pretty dress she said was made of rayon. It was soft and flowery patterned. All of her dresses were of the same style and had a smell of talcum powder. Aunt Lyda and Grandma had a running rivalry over who was the prettiest. Aunt Lyda accused Grandma of ratting her hair to make it look fuller, but Grandma denied this. Bonnie thought Grandma was the prettiest and told her so. "I'm the youngest one," Grandma said, and Bonnie could tell she thought she was the prettiest despite her one glass eye. Mama said Grandma had gotten an infection in her eye when she arrived in the United States and the doctor had to take it out. Bonnie thought that must have been terrible.

Aunt Lyda served a dish called succotash, made from green lima beans and corn. There was a dessert called jam tarts. They were made from left-over pie dough, cut into rounds with a glass and sandwiched together with red jelly. The top round had a small circle cut into it so the jelly would show through. Bonnie liked it all, but Annie didn't try much. That seemed to be okay with Aunt Lyda, and no one spanked her for not eating.

At night before bedtime, Grandma always gave the girls two stewed prunes swimming in their juice in a little saucer. The juice was a bit too sweet for Bonnie, but she finished it all. It seemed to be important to Grandma and Bonnie wanted to please her. Then it was up the stairs to Grandma's bedroom. They slept in the same bed with her. The last thing Grandma did before getting into bed was remove her glass eye. She would put it into a little cup of liquid on the floor beside the bed. Bonnie wondered how Grandma popped it out of her eye. Did it hurt? Poor Grandma, getting that infection.

Annie was nervous about looking at Grandma asleep, with one eye closed and the other just an open dark hole. "I'm scared, Bonnie," she whispered, "What if the eye comes after me?"

"Don't be afraid," Bonnie whispered back. She reached over and poked into the cup, stirring the glass eye around a little. "See, it can't get out," she said. That made Annie giggle, and they both pulled the covers over their heads so Grandma wouldn't wake up from the noise.

Althea Nordstrom lived on the other side, in the house to the east of Grandma and Grandpa Johnson's. She liked to play with Bonnie and Annie. She had a Sears-Roebuck catalogue, and on each page, she had inserted a set of different paper dolls and their cut-out clothes. "This keeps the dolls separate," she explained, "and it keeps the clothes from getting mixed up with the other dolls." She let Bonnie and Annie play with some of them. Bonnie was thrilled. It was fun to make up stories with the dolls. The only paper dolls she had were the ones cut out from the *Brenda Star* comic strip in Grandma Smith's Sunday paper. Althea's dolls were cut out from real paper doll books purchased from the dime store.

There were so many choices—Bonita Granville, Deanna Durbin, Judy Garland. Bonnie's favorite among the dolls in the Sears Catalogue pages were the *Dionne Quintuplets* and Annie liked the *Shirley Temple* doll. Their paper outfits had tags around the shoulders to fasten them onto the dolls and were so lovely. There were clothes for all of the seasons. Even mittens, boots, and caps.

Bonnie slipped one of the quintuplet dolls under her dress. She felt a thrill of excitement when she took the doll. She liked to look at it when she was alone. She thought the dolls name was Marie. She wondered if Althea ever missed her. One day she saw her looking frantically through the pages of the catalogue.

"I can't find one of the Quintuplets" she said to Bonnie.

"Have you looked on every page, Althea? There's over a thousand pages in the book." Bonnie decided not to say anything, and she tore up the Marie doll after that, then put the pieces into Grandma's iron kitchen stove, burning her fingers a little while lifting the lid.

Sometimes they played in Althea's garage, Old Maid and Rummy mostly. Another boy from down the street named Peter often joined them. He had a hard time walking because he had a club foot. He wore a special shoe, and he didn't seem to mind taking it off and showing the girls his oddly shaped foot. Bonnie felt a strange attraction to him. She thought him so handsome. He taught them a game called Spin the Bottle. Where the bottle stopped, the person spinning had to kiss the one it pointed to.

There was much giggling, but no one kissed. Peter was older, and he showed them how to do a proper kiss. He held out his hand and demonstrated how to put one's lips slowly onto the back of the hand, near the thumb where it was softer, and make a smacking noise. They all tried it until he said, "Now you have it right." Bonnie liked that game better than Rummy.

When Peter would leave, limping with his funny gait, Bonnie followed him with her eyes until he reached his house. *Maybe he was a prince in disguise and a kiss would make him whole*, she thought. She wanted to go with him and try out the proper kiss.

It was quite a wonderful summer, sometimes on the front lawn playing jack knife with real knives. Annie and Bonnie sat opposite each other on the grass, tossing the knives with open blades into the air where they spun around and fell back to the ground. If the knife stuck in the ground with the handle upright, it counted for five points. It was a daring game, even dangerous, but fun all the same. Even more exciting were the sewing needles, Bonnie's name for the clouds of dragonflies, darting over their heads. She told Annie that they would sew her fingers together if she wasn't careful.

And it was nice to sit with Grandma on the front porch learning to sew and crochet. Bonnie could make lace pineapples, but Annie just made little lumps of thread all twisted together. "Her hands are still too small," Grandma said. She just nodded at Bonnie's efforts. *Grandma likes Annie better*, she thought. *I wish I knew why.*

When it was almost time to go, Bonnie heard that Daddy had gotten a job in a place called Crystal Falls, Michigan. He had gotten it through a program President Roosevelt started called the Work Project Association, also known as the WPA, He was going to be a band director. Bonnie could tell by Mama's voice that she was pleased about this. Crystal Falls. *What a magical name,* thought Bonnie. It was seventy miles from Marquette, an unimaginable distance.

Bonnie felt bad about leaving. Crystal Falls was even farther from Negaunee, which meant probably no more summers with Grandma and Grandpa Johnson. Grandma took them to a picnic before they left. All her Swedish friends were there. The food was so good, the cabbage rolls especially. Uncle Lemmy, and his Italian wife, Violet, weren't there, but their son Roy came.

Roy was a chubby boy and a little mean. He had brown curly hair and wore short pants and a sailor shirt. He was Grandma Johnson's second grandchild, and, unlike his Italian mother, he was accepted. Uncle Lemmy just dropped Roy off because Grandma still hadn't accepted Violet. Bonnie saw Violet once when she and Grandma were downtown by the Mather Inn. She thought Violet looked so pretty, wearing bright lipstick, her long dark hair pulled back into a snood. She wore a red dress with ruffles which clung to her body. Grandma said, "That's Violet," but she didn't speak to her.

"We're going to see your Great-grandmother Nelson," Grandma said after the picnic. She wants to see you before you leave for Crystal Falls. She's old and doesn't leave her house. She speaks only Swedish." They walked several blocks to Bonnie's great-grandmother's house. Aunt Lyda came, too, and Lyda's daughter, Evelyn. "Evelyn is your second cousin," Grandma Johnson explained. She works in another town, Ishpeming, and she lives there, too. She's visiting her mother for the week."

They formed a parade—Grandma, Auntie, and Evelyn in single file. The sidewalks were narrow, and in some places roots raised the concrete squares, so they had to be careful. Bonnie and Annie held hands, walking behind the entourage.

Great-grandmother's house was small, but very neat. They sat around a little round table on straight chairs. Great-grandmother told them to sit down in Swedish. She had a glass pitcher filled with tea. Grandma Johnson poured it into tall glasses all around, saying the pitcher was too heavy for her mother to lift. Bonnie tried the drink. She had never had tea before. It was tepid and tasted awful. She and Annie made faces at each other as the adults carried on a conversation in Swedish.

Great-grandmother was tiny. Her hair was grey and pulled back into a little knot at the nape of her neck. Bonnie could see her bare skull through the hair. *She's almost bald*, Bonnie thought.

There was only one picture on the wall of the living room, of a handsome man with a fat mustache. "That's your great-grandfather," Grandma Johnson said. "He died shortly after arriving in the United States. Lyda and I came with them when I was a young girl. I grew up in this house. We took in laundry and sewing." *No wonder Grandma was so good at sewing*, Bonnie thought.

Great-grandmother beckoned her and Annie to come to her before they left. She put her hand on each of their heads and murmured something in Swedish. Bonnie thought it was something important. "She's giving you her blessing," Grandma said. "We have to leave now as she's getting tired."

Bonnie remembered feeling connected to something from another world far away, something big and mysterious.

Crystal Falls, Michigan
1937-1939

Chapter 10

The house Daddy found for them was on High Street. It was the biggest place Bonnie had ever lived in. It was on a corner lot with a woody area on one side. Bonnie took the measure of the place. There was a bathroom with a sink and stool, but there was no hot water or bath tub.

There was an empty, always cold, spare room and two bedrooms, one of which the three children were to sleep in.

They had to take their baths in a wash tub which Mama filled with warm water from the kitchen stove. The oval tin tub was placed on the kitchen table. Everyone took turns in the bathing water—Augie first, then Annie, then Bonnie, and finally Mama and Daddy. This happened every Saturday night before Daddy went out on a playing job.

"You're turn, Bonnie, c'mon, before the water gets too cold," Mama said. Bonnie was ready, standing naked, as Annie was lifted out of the washtub and wrapped in a ragged towel, her pajamas near a small electric heater. Mama lifted Bonnie into the tepid grey water and quickly soaped her all over, even her hair, then dunked her under to give a final rinse. The kids got into their pajamas in the front room while Mama and Daddy took their turn. Bonnie had to help Augie with his.

The living room had a couch and chair and best of all an old upright piano. Bonnie loved the piano, even though there were a few keys missing at the very bottom. She only used the keys in the middle, anyway. One day, as she was picking at the keys, Daddy called, "Helen, come here. She's playing a tune." Even Mama, who had an uncertain ear, recognized the song, *When I Grow Too Old to Dream*. Bonnie knew the words, too, and sang them as she played. She had been a bit wary of her father so she felt glad that he seemed pleased and she played it again, using only one finger all the while.

The piano had other uses, too—the bench, that is. It was moved to the table at meal times for the kids to sit on, as the table had only two chairs. The bench also served as a medical table when Bonnie's baby teeth became loose, and that's where she was held down, tears streaming, as Daddy tied a string around a tooth and yanked it from its socket. She bled a little and Mama put a piece of toilet paper rolled up in a wad over the hole to stop the bleeding.

In the house on High Street the back door opened to a long porch supported on stilts. Several steps led down to a garden area. There was a large plot where Daddy planted potatoes in the ground and string beans hidden in leaves that climbed on poles; they were called pole beans and they grew especially long, as long as a pencil and even fatter. There were dozens on each pole. Mama had to cut them in four pieces for cooking. They were stringy and tough for eating.

Daddy gave Bonnie and Annie tin cans filled with a bit of kerosene. Their job was to pick potato bugs from the plant leaves and drop them into the kerosene. The bugs were slimy, but it was a satisfying task, watching the bugs shrivel and die when they hit the kerosene. Crawling through the rows, they often dug down with their fingers to see how the potatoes were coming along. Daddy had planted pieces of potato with long white eyes on them, and now they were changing into clusters of small yellow baby potatoes. Daddy sent Bonnie with some of the harvest over to the priest's house. His housekeeper never turned anything away.

The Church of the Holy Angels was kitty-corner from their house and Daddy had the family attending Mass there every Sunday, sitting in the front pew. This building was nothing like the cathedral in Marquette. It was small and low-ceilinged in the basement floor. People said there was no money to finish the main floor because of the Depression.

"Are we still Catholic here, Daddy?" Bonnie asked.

"Yes Bonnie, Of course you're a Catholic. It was burned onto your soul when you were baptized."

Here, Bonnie made her first communion along with several other seven-year-old boys and girls. She took instructions from Father Penry. To be pure and holy enough to receive the Body and Blood of Christ, she would first have to confess her sins. There were mortal sins and venial sins. Father Penry explained how to discover these sins through an examination of conscience. The children were to kneel in the church and think about what bad things they had done.

Father Penry stood before the children, and said in a quiet voice, "We'll go through the commandments, and you'll ask yourself if you've disobeyed them in any way," He went through a possible list of sins for some time. "Did you tell a lie? Did you steal? Did you say a bad word?" Then he went into the confessional box at the back of the church to wait for each child to approach individually.

Thinking of her sins was a difficult task for Bonnie. She knew her prayers; the Our Father, Hail Mary, Angel of God and Glory Be, had been drilled into her over and over by the Sisters at the Cathedral School. And now there was a new one to be memorized—the Act of Contrition. How were prayers supposed to reveal her sins? She recalled things that were called "bad" by her parents, and at last a list started to form in her head. Augie had knocked a book from her hand while she was reading and she had slapped him and made him cry. He ran to Mama and told her.

"Bonnie, don't hit your little brother. He's only five."

"I didn't hit him, Mama. He's just saying that. He fell while he was pulling a book from me, and he even ripped two of the pages."

So, she had told a lie, two even. Was that a mortal or a venial sin? There was the time in Marquette when she was playing in the sand lot with another boy, and they had both pulled down their pants to see the different way that boys and girls go potty. That must have been a sin, too, because Mama told her and Annie never to look at or touch themselves "there" or they would go insane. Another sin.

Bonnie was glad she had something to tell Father Penry while she was in the small, dark curtained box, kneeling on a hard step before the priest who was in his cubical with a grilled window so that he couldn't see who the sinner was. She could make out his ear against the dividing screen and hoped it was true that he couldn't see her. "Bless me, Father for I have sinned" and she went down her list.

"I lied twice, I was mean to my sister, and I pulled my pants down in front of a boy." She left the worst until last and ended with "That's all Father."

"Say your Act of Contrition," he said. As soon as she finished the prayer, he quickly mumbled words of absolution in Latin, followed by "Go, your sins are forgiven. Sin no more. For your penance say three Our Fathers and three Hail Marys."

She left the box. Other boys and girls were lined up down the aisle—she had been the first in line—waiting for their turn to be forgiven. As she knelt to say the penance, she remembered another day when she had been throwing rocks at the mean kids across the street, even managing to hit one of them. Another sin. She had lied to the priest when he asked, "Is that all?" "Yes, Father," she had answered. She didn't feel forgiven, only guilty, as she left the church to return home.

"Did you make your First Confession?" Daddy asked.

"Yes, Daddy, is that all we need to do?"

"No, Bonnie, Catholics do this each Saturday so they can receive Holy Communion on Sunday. Tomorrow you'll make your very first Holy Communion. You must have nothing to eat or drink in the morning, so that you're pure inside to receive the Body and Blood of Christ. He'll be present in a wafer, which the priest will put on your tongue. You mustn't chew the host, but swallow it whole." *How is this possible?* Bonnie wondered. Her imagination could not grasp the idea that the thin host could be the Body and Blood of Jesus.

She wore a pretty white dress—her first not made of flour sacks—that her mother had borrowed from a lady that played in Daddy's band. Her head was covered with a white veil, a new one bought from the J.C. Penny store. Even her shoes and stockings were white. They were new, too. Daddy told Mama to spend the money.

"It's a special day, Helen. You wouldn't understand," he said.

Bonnie felt like a movie star. She hoped she was pure enough. As she knelt at the altar railing the next morning and stuck out her tongue for the wafer, she kept thinking about the sin she had forgotten to confess.

The thought of going to hell kept intruding as she moved the dry host around in her mouth, then to the back of her tongue, and finally down her throat. She managed to quell the uncertain feeling of damnation and was thankful that she hadn't bitten Jesus before He came into her heart.

Since this was now going to take place every week, though not in a white dress, Bonnie resolved to commit some small sins so that she would have something to tell the priest. Nothing mortal, though, like killing or cursing. Talking back to Mama, or telling little lies, or stealing something small would do the trick.

There were only two pictures from these years, one of Mama and Daddy and the three kids standing near a newer car, another Ford, a Model A. Daddy's hand is atop Augie's head in a protective manner, and Bonnie and Annie are on either side of Mama. The other photo is of Daddy standing with a baton in his hand as the director of the WPA band. Bonnie was proud of her father, thinking him important. Her family, she thought, must be important, too.

Her mother looks so pretty in the picture, wearing some sort of fur stole around her shoulders. She said Aunt Tilly had given it to her when they left Marquette. Aunt Tilly now lived in a *good* neighborhood in Marquette because she had gone to the Normal School for two years, was a teacher, and better than that, had married a local optometrist. Uncle Walfred didn't want her to work, so she didn't. He was a doctor, after all.

Once Mama and the girls were invited to an afternoon party at Aunt Tilly's house. Bonnie liked the large spray of wax flowers before the fireplace. It was so big, covering the whole opening where the fire was supposed to be lit, but Aunt Tilly said they never lit it because of the mess it would make.

In the Crystal Falls house, the heat came from a furnace in the basement. A truck came every so often and dumped a ton of coal down a chute, through a window under the back porch; "Soft coal," her daddy said, "because it's cheaper."

"It makes so much dirt," Mama said. She was clean crazy; even a piece of paper on the floor would set her off. "This place is a mess," she would complain.

The family saved money on food, too, using the potatoes, beans, and tomatoes from the garden. Bonnie and Annie often pulled a wagon to a building a few blocks away, where they were given oranges, macaroni, and cans of carrots and peas. President Roosevelt's helpers gave these out. Mama said the helpers were part of the WPA, just like Daddy. Mama saved potato water and used it to make rolls, which were so good, warm, buttered with salad dressing.

One day Bonnie saw Daddy carrying Mama out the front door. Her dress was soaked with blood, and it was running down the steps. He lifted her into the car and drove off. A lady named Phyllis came to stay with them. Daddy was gone for three days. He came home, looking worried. "I've been at the hospital with Mama," he said. "She needs our prayers. The doctor is not giving me much hope." The family all knelt and prayed for her so she wouldn't die. She didn't.

When she came home—after the longest time—she had a new baby with her. She called him Alan. The lady from the county, Phyllis, stayed to help, coming every day for six weeks until Mama got stronger. She said Mama wouldn't be having any more babies, since the doctor had said, "Enough was enough," and he had done something to make sure this wouldn't happen again.

Phyllis liked to fix Mama's hair, rolling the sides up like the movie stars she saw pictured in magazines. "Helen, you look prettier than ever" she always said. Mama liked the magazines, too, but Daddy didn't. He didn't approve. Mama kept a stash of the movie star magazines under her bed. Bonnie knew where they were, and she studied them carefully when no one was around. This was another good sin for confession.

Two happy things happened during these years. The first was the discovery of an uncle of Daddy's who ran the local movie theater. Uncle Gordon—that was his name—told Daddy the Smith family could attend the movies for nothing! They only had to pay the two-penny tax. This gave Mama a break every Saturday. Bonnie oversaw the trip downtown, and she took Annie and Augie in hand as they walked down a big hill to the theater. She reached up to the ticket window and gave the lady six cents, two cents for each person, announcing proudly, "Our Uncle Gordon owns this theater." Sometimes the ticket lady didn't look so happy. After all, Uncle Gordon lived in another town in Wisconsin, where he owned a few other theaters. She let them pass, though.

Daddy had to approve whatever movie was playing, checking his list of motion pictures put out by the Catholic Church to see if they were suitable for children. That usually worked out, because Saturday afternoons were pictures about cowboys, Flash Gordon serials, cartoons, and The Three Stooges. Everyone laughed so hard at the funny parts that their stomachs hurt. There was a lot of noise and spitball throwing during the talking or singing parts of the cowboy shows. Augie always hid under the seat when the shooting began.

Augie got sick around that time. He had a high fever, and the county nurse came to the house several times during his illness. He laid still on the hard couch, covered with a small yellow blanket, sometimes moaning, and he hardly ate or drank. He was a rather chubby child when the sickness started, but after a few weeks he turned into a thin little boy. He never got his fat back. Bonnie didn't know what the sickness was. Her mother kept putting cold washcloths on his head and stomach and she would start to cry when Daddy came from work. Bonnie felt scared inside until Augie got better.

The other happy thing was the school. It was a public school. Daddy was unhappy about this. Bonnie was overjoyed. There was no more "Good morning, Sister," or jumping to her feet when another sister entered the room. No phonics either, just story reading or numbers. The teacher, Mrs. Hill held contests, pitting boys against girls. She put arithmetic problems on the chalk board to see who could add numbers the fastest. A lot of times Bonnie won, and she felt a sense of satisfaction when this occurred. She even enjoyed the surge of tension during the contest. She liked winning.

Mrs. Hill was heavy, wore a lot of red rouge on her face and had a bosom that covered her belt. Kids joked about this enormous top part of her body.

In third grade, she had Mrs. Bean. Mrs. Bean was pretty. All the girls wanted to be like Mrs. Bean. Mrs. Bean taught a class of singing every day. The kids would put their pens and paper into their desks, which opened at the top. "Take out your singing book" Mrs. Bean would say at the appointed time—every day at two o'clock. That was Bonnie's favorite time in the school day. Mrs. Bean often gave her a part to sing alone.

One day she was picked to go to the Rotary meeting at the local hotel. She sang a song called *Sunbonnet Sally* while standing before the men in the meeting room. It was at night. Bonnie wore a sunbonnet and a fancy apron, and her cheeks were rouged. She felt glamorous, like a movie star. Her hair was braided on the sides and the braids were pulled back and fastened with a big bow. The bonnet covered her big ear. Her mother had used rags the night before to curl her hair. The rags were hard to sleep on, tied in their knots, but the resulting curls were amazing. "You have to suffer for beauty," her mother said. She had read the part about suffering in one of her movie magazines.

Bonnie sang her song in a loud clear voice. Mrs. Bean smiled at her when she finished the song. *I was nervous before I started*, she thought, *but I liked doing it. The men liked it, too. They clapped and laughed a lot.* She liked being in the limelight.

Part of the school day was spent learning cursive. There was an inkwell on her desk, and she dipped her pen point into the ink, then moved it to the triple lined paper, trying not to drip. Bonnie moved the pen around in interlocking circles—or slanted right—with upward and downward strokes across the paper. Finally, she formed these strokes into letters—small a's and capital A's —working her way through the alphabet. She practiced writing her name over and over. Bonnie Smith., Bonnie, Bonnie, Bonnie, Smith. Smith, Smith. This was who she was.

The school had a play yard with swings and slides, where recess was held when the weather allowed. Near the hard-surfaced yard was a wooded area where some of the kids—boys—would sneak off and do bad stuff like swear or talk about girls' underpants.

Stairs and a brick wall formed one corner of the school building and served as a private place for Bonnie. She would stand in that corner with one hand on the wall and one hand on the side of the staircase. Then she could feel her feet rise from the ground, and she would release her hands, remaining suspended in the air, until she became nervous about getting too high and would drop back to the ground. No one saw her seeming to float in the air and she never told anyone. *Who can I tell*, she thought. *My mother? Annie? Who would believe me? They would laugh and say I was making things up. Maybe I've dreamed it myself. No, It's my own special power. My own magic.* But it didn't always work. Especially if she tried to make it happen, and one day she gave up trying and avoided that corner of the building.

Sometimes the school had fire drills. From a big open window on the second floor everyone got to slide down a long white tube that looked something like a fat caterpillar. The tube ran all the way to the ground. Bonnie, liked this exercise, whooping, and hollering all the way down.

Getting to school was another matter. One of the houses Bonnie had to pass had a bulldog behind a low fence. It always came running and barking fiercely when she walked by. This was the way she was told to go, as it was the quickest. She dreaded that part of the walk. What if the dog got loose and came after her? She was afraid of dogs.

Daddy once brought a puppy home when they were living in Marquette. The puppy liked to nip at Bonnie's feet. This scared her, and she would jump on top of the kitchen table, screaming. The puppy seemed as big as the horses in her nightmare.

"Don't be afraid, he won't hurt you. He just wants to play," Daddy said as he took the puppy in his arms. Still, she didn't like the nipping, and finally the puppy was given to a neighbor two blocks over.

Chapter 11

Crystal Falls was a place where Bonnie learned to roller skate. The metal skates were fastened to her shoes with a key. Back and forth on the sidewalk she sped, enjoying the feeling of flying, a freedom even better than the levitation she had experienced at the school.

She now had a best friend, Rita Larson, who skated alongside her. Sometimes they held hands as they skated or walked together to school. They told each other everything about their lives. Rita went to Sunday school at her church and she described the fun they had during church services in a separate room, away from their parents, coloring bible pictures, singing Bible songs, and having treats to eat. Bonnie wanted to go Rita's church with her on Sundays, but Daddy said no. "The Larsons are not Catholic and they can't go to heaven."

Bonnie was now starting to think of Daddy as Father, strict Father, and Father with a razor strap which he used to sharpen his blades for shaving, and sometimes for spanking. Augie got the most spankings. He was always in some sort of trouble, for things like stealing marbles or hitting Annie.

Mama had to be on the lookout at night because Augie liked to take off his clothes and wander around inside the house, sometimes outside. Mama said he was a sleepwalker. Daddy was no help watching Augie because he was gone many nights, playing piano in local bars to earn extra money. It was all on Mama.

One of their neighbors was Officer McGinty, a state police officer. He was the father of another of Bonnie's playmates, Mary Beth. Bonnie was always afraid he would come and take Augie away when Augie was out wandering at night, bare naked.

Bonnie was on her best behavior when at the McGinty's. Mary Beth often invited Bonnie and Annie over to play under their dining room table. The table was covered with a big blanket so it was like a tent, hiding them from the outside world. Mary Beth had small doll dishes which they laid out on the rug and pretended to have coffee, drinking daintily from the empty cups. It was their own little house.

Sometimes her mother, Mrs. McGinty, would bring out cupcakes from the kitchen, but they had to have them on top of the table. Mrs. McGinty was a petite, quiet lady. Bonnie supposed she was afraid of Officer McGinty too. Once she had heard her screaming for a short time when Officer McGinty was at home. Bonnie always knew when he was home because his police car was parked in their driveway.

Rita Larson was never invited to the McGinty's. Mary Beth said it was because the Larson boys were always in trouble with the local police. Bonnie liked the Larson brothers, especially John. They ran a bait selling business from their garage. John let Bonnie take a flashlight on their lawn in the evenings after a rain, so she could pull out the night crawlers from the wet grass and put them into a tin can filled with dirt.

The wriggly worms even crawled on the sidewalks and were squished or dried up if they didn't get back under the ground when the sun came out. The Larson boys sold them to local fishermen for five cents a can, ten worms to a can. Bonnie got a nickel or a dime for helping. She liked money, and decided to get a lot of it someday.

"Did you ever dream of being rich, Rita? I mean really rich?" she asked her friend.

"Not often," said Rita. "My father said we have all we could ever need."

Rita's father worked for the town of Crystal Falls. Their family had never had to move. Bonnie's mother said a city job as was for life. "Those jobs are hard to get," she said. You have to know someone."

"Doesn't Daddy know someone?" Bonnie asked. "He's a band director, Mama. Lots of people know him."

Not the right someone, Bonnie. That's all I can tell you," said Mama.

Mama was a chain smoker and didn't get out of the house much as the new baby, Alan, was too small to leave alone. She sent Bonnie to the gas station every afternoon after school—snow or rain—to buy her cigarettes—Marvels, eleven cents a pack. Another errand was going to the post office, where she told the clerk, "Two threes, please," handing over six cents, as she was instructed to do. Then she was given two three-cent stamps, in an envelope so she wouldn't lose them. The worst job was going to the drug store to buy Kotex. She had no idea what this was for, but she sensed there was something secret and shameful about this box of twelve thick pads, and she would run quickly home with this clumsy, never wrapped box under her arm.

Father Penry was the pocket money guy. Whenever he was standing outside the priest's house, Bonnie, Rita, and Annie would gather around him, laughing at his stories and grabbing at his pants legs until he produced a nickel for each of them.

Then they would go off to the Blue Link, a little store tucked away behind the gas station, to buy candy cigarettes or paper rolls with small candies stuck on them, or little wax pop bottles, filled with sweet colored liquid, that they sucked out of the top, then chewed the wax until all the sweet taste was gone, then spit it out onto the grass, in a contest to see who could spit it the farthest. They talked about the boys having contests too, in the woods near the school, competing to see could whizz their piss stream the farthest.

One day, a man dressed as a soldier came to their school and said, "Collect foil for the government." That started a frenzy of kids searching alleys and streets for used gum wrappers, from which they carefully peeled the silvery foil from the paper backing. Bonnie was diligent at this, at last collecting enough foil to form a huge ball. Kids met and compared the sizes of their treasure. Bonnie's was the biggest. "What shall we do with these?" she asked Rita. "How do we get them to the government?" Rita didn't know, nor did anyone else she asked. Not even her mother.

"Just get rid of it," Mama said "It's filthy dirty. I don't want it in the house." Bonnie didn't know what became of it, only that one day it was gone. *Maybe the government didn't need foil as much as that man at school had said*, Bonnie thought.

Chapter 12

It took a long time for Mama to recover from Alan's birth.

"She had her children too close together", the dentist said, "Her teeth are soft because she's lost her bone calcium." He pulled all of them out, in stages, first the top teeth, then the bottom ones, then he made her some new ones. They were hard to fit because of her crooked jaw. Mama said they hurt and made sores in her mouth as they slipped around when she ate. Bonnie cringed when she saw the bloody gums and the look of pain on her mother's face.

Mama's legs bothered her, too. She showed Bonnie the blue, pulsing veins that ran behind her knees. "Please be good, and stop fighting with Augie," she cried. "I can't stand the racket." Bonnie had another sin for the Saturday confessions: fighting with her brother and sister and making her mother cry. Her sin litany was growing.

Alan was baptized in the Holy Angel Church. Mama did go that time. It was the only time Bonnie could remember her coming with the rest of the family. Florence and Freddie Matusik were the Godparents, chosen by Daddy. Daddy said they were good Catholics, and Freddie played in the WPA band. Florence did, too. Freddie played the sax and Florence played the clarinet. Mama and Phyllis talked about Florence, saying things like "She dyes her hair too black," "her lipstick looks smeared on," and "she's so loud."

One day Freddie and Florence stopped by their house in Freddie's car. Mama went out to talk to Florence while Freddie was going over things with Daddy inside the house. Bonnie was standing by, listening, while Mama and Florence were laughing and talking in the friendliest way. She felt important standing there and wanted to be part of the grown-up conversation. "My Mama doesn't like you." she broke in.

Things got awkward after that, and Mama said, "She doesn't know who she's talking about. She means Peggy in the trumpet section. Peggy is such a gossip. Of course, I like you and Freddie so much. You're our best friends."

Bonnie knew she had talked out of turn, but she was surprised that her mama had told such a lie. She felt her mother's disapproval enveloping her. She decided that from then on, she would keep her own secrets from Mama. She would tread carefully around her, not knowing what Mama might tell others about Bonnie's comings and goings. Only Rita—and sometimes Annie—would be privy to her real life.

"You mustn't interrupt adults when they are in conversation," was the only thing Mama mentioned after the incident. She didn't look directly at Bonnie when she said this while moving to the play pen to pick up Alan who was crying.

Uncle Gordon, who owned the movie theater, had a wife and daughter. He and Aunt Joan and Cousin Jackie dropped by one day from Wisconsin driving a long black car. Uncle Gordon said it used to be a hearse. Jackie was a big woman, enormous really. She weighed over three hundred pounds. She was Aunt Joan's and Uncle Gordon's only child. Joan told Mama that Jackie had had a terrible fever as a child and they had to pack her in ice in the bath tub for twenty-four hours.

When she recovered, she started to eat everything and still couldn't stop eating. "I have to feed her a dozen eggs a day," said Aunt Joan. "She loves mashed potatoes, a whole peck, with gravy. Then she downs at least a dozen ears of corn. She loves chocolate cake, too. We drive the hearse so she can have a place to lie down when we travel. We don't travel much, as you can imagine."

Bonnie listened to this story in quiet amazement. She didn't want to get that enormous. Cousin Jackie had a sweet face, though it could hardly be seen, smothered by the many fat rolls under her chin. She didn't get out of the car, merely waved to Mama and Bonnie from her lying position. Bonnie could see that her legs were all rolly, too, but her feet were tiny, shod in soft blue slippers.

Bonnie resolved to watch her eating. She had been hiding forbidden candy in her private dresser drawer. She gave most of it to Annie and Augie and even a tiny piece to Alan, who was finally beginning to walk and had a few baby teeth. The relatives from Wisconsin stayed for just a short while, and then left in their hearse. Bonnie never saw them again.

President Roosevelt closed the WPA band project after Bonnie finished the third grade. The weekly concerts in the park had been so much fun. There was always free cream soda and potato chips. There was a lot of running around, trying to get away from the boys. The kids didn't sit around listening to the music, only the big people, and there were the picnics at the falls. There really was a Crystal Falls, with water splashing down onto rocks below a high drop that was lit up in soft colors during the summer time. Maybe it wasn't a high drop, but to Bonnie it seemed to be. She loved the magic of it. She wanted to live in Crystal Falls forever.

During this time, Bonnie had made some progress with the piano. Daddy had enrolled her in the school band, letting her use his trumpet. She hated trying to play the instrument; such hard work blowing into the mouthpiece, and her lips were so sore after a practice session, but she did learn where middle 'C' was on the music staff, and Daddy showed her where it was on the piano keys.

A spell fell over her at that time, and she saw the dots on the staff start to reveal themselves to her, and she realized she could play songs from the music paper. She stayed at the piano for such a long time. *I've found another language; I love this so much*, she thought. Bonnie had found her first love. The piano keys quickly became an extension of her fingers, her arms, and her heart and head. Sometimes when she was playing she even forgot about wanting to be rich.

Songs sounded sour when she tried to play the music with her left and right hand together. Her mother noticed her struggle, even though she herself couldn't carry a tune. She explained to Bonnie that the dots for the left-hand music on the staff had to be played three notes higher than the right-hand notes. Bonnie was glad Grandma Johnson had made Mama take piano lessons. She still didn't trust her mother after she'd told the lie in front of her, but she respected her in that matter because it worked. She also told Daddy she wouldn't play the trumpet any more. "I like the piano, Daddy, it's more fun," she told him. She was afraid of hurting his feelings because he played the trumpet sometimes at his gigs.

He said, "Okay, honey. Maybe Augie will take it up when he gets big enough. Don't worry about it."

When Bonnie heard they were going to move back to Marquette—into Grandma Smith's house—Bonnie didn't want to leave. "Please, Mama, can't we stay here? I love it in Crystal Falls," she begged over and over.

"Daddy's job is done here. He's been called back to the Piqua. We have to move and stay at Grandma's house, just for a while," Mama answered, trying to console her.

Bonnie ran to Rita's house. "We have to move. I don't want to." They held onto each other.

"Let's go to our place," Rita said.

They ran down a grassy hill leading to a railroad track. They had often gone there to watch the trains and share their secrets. It was their private place. They made promises to each other never to forget their friendship, and to think of each other every night before going to sleep. They sat there a long time, arms entwined, weeping.

Chapter 13

Marquette, Michigan
1940

Grandpa Smith had died while they were living in Crystal Falls. Grandma told Daddy the story of his passing. Grandpa had contracted pneumonia and was taken to St. Luke's Hospital. Grandma Marie said that when the priest had come to give him the last sacrament of Extreme Unction and administer Holy Communion, the Communion wafer had leaped from the priest's hand and landed right on Grandpa's tongue, where it melted, vanishing before her eyes. Others gathered around his bed praying, saw it too. Aunt Tilly had cried out, "It's a miracle." Uncle Francis was there, too, but he had pooh-poohed the whole thing.

This story puzzled Bonnie. *Grandma Smith wouldn't make this up*, she thought. *Maybe the wafer is the Body and Blood of Christ. I'll be more careful about recalling my sins every Saturday; I'm terrified of going to Hell.* She faithfully recited her Act of Contrition every night, occasionally even kneeling by the bed if the floor wasn't too cold.

New things seemed to be happening so quickly. She rarely thought of Rita and Crystal Falls. It was still summer, and now she, Annie, and Augie could walk alone to Fortune Lake for swimming. Annie and Augie had to stay near the shore, but Bonnie found she could stay afloat in the water by paddling with her arms and kicking with her feet, while keeping her head under water. She felt safe if she could safely touch the sandy bottom with her big toe, raising her head above water for a breath after each short forward propulsion.

She had gone on like this for a while one afternoon, feeling triumphant with this new-found ability, until her feet suddenly felt nothing but water when she tried to stand. She began to panic. The lifeguard must have noticed, for the next thing she knew she was being pulled toward shore. His arm was around her chest, holding her head above water all the while. She felt confused and at the same time embarrassed at having to be rescued.

"Don't go past the ropes," he said, "and keep closer to shore." She disliked the shore line because there were so many blood suckers. The suckers would attach themselves to her feet and ankles. When she, Annie, and Augie were in the changing house, she had to pull the suckers off them and herself, and hurl them into the sand outside. Some of the boys had little bags of salt which they sprinkled onto the suckers, laughing as the ugly leeches shriveled up.

Swimming was more fun when Aunt Lillian took them on a longer walk to the shore of Lake Superior. A picture shows Bonnie wearing a suit that had been one of her aunt's. It hangs loosely from her shoulders, the bra cups draping helplessly like deflated balloons. The picture is in black and white, but she remembers—the suit was blue.

Lake Superior water was always ice cold, even in summer. It was shallow near shore, and Bonnie could wade out to the numerous rocky outcroppings where small bushes grew, some of them with blueberries on them and some covered with little hard red berries.

"Don't eat the red ones," Lillian called. "They're poisonous. They'll make you sick." Bonnie couldn't resist trying one and then quickly spit it out. It tasted so bitter, maybe it *was* poisonous.

The beach was near high iron ore docks. Aunt Lillian said Daddy was a wonderful swimmer. When he was a boy, he and his friends used to dive straight down from the very top of the docks. Daddy stopped doing this when his friend, Ralph, fell short during a dive, hitting the steel outcropping near the bottom of the dock and was killed. Though Daddy stopped the diving after that accident, he still liked to frighten everyone when he swam underwater for the longest time, never seeming to come up for air. Bonnie always held her breath, too, until he reappeared.

"Where's Daddy," she asked Aunt Lillian. "Why doesn't he come up?"

And then there he would be, head above the water, waving at her. "He's playing the possum game," her aunt said. "He does the dead man's float, too. "He'll never grow up." Bonnie hated that game.

Aunt Lillian was so beautiful, with her thick, auburn, wavy hair, and long red fingernails, her looks only a bit marred by her rather long nose, which she had inherited from her father, Grandpa Ollie. She was already eighteen years old, ten years older than Bonnie. Bonnie adored her. Lillian liked to lie on her towel on the white beach sand, turning every so often to achieve the perfect tan.

Whenever Aunt Lillian was in Grandma's kitchen with her friends, Olga, and Betty, fixing each other's hair and painting one another's toenails, and smoking cigarettes from long cigarette holders, Bonnie stood nearby, wishing she could be part of this ritual.

Sometimes Aunt Lillian would fix Bonnie's hair, too. Bonnie tried to see the results in the mirror over the kitchen sink, but couldn't, even if she jumped up. Lillian would lift her so she could see. She didn't like when her aunt fixed her hair behind her ears, because then she would notice her one protruding ear. *I can never wear pigtails*, she thought, sadly.

Once Aunt Lillian cut Bonnie's hair too short. Frustrated by the fact that her one ear was now always visible, thanks to Aunt Lillian, Bonnie took one of her aunt's cigarette holders that had been left lying on the kitchen table and kept it for some time in her pick-up-sticks box. She took pleasure in the theft, until, fearing discovery, she put it amongst some things in her aunt's bottom dresser drawer. Bonnie excused this sin of stealing because she had put it back. It was not, she decided, a matter for confession.

Aunt Lillian's friends wore ankle bracelets and dangly earrings. They seemed to always be jingling as they laughed and chatted about boys. They were adept with their cigarettes, too. They rolled golden tobacco strands from small cans into special thin papers, wetting the papers closed with their tongues. Pieces of tobacco would sometimes stick to their lips as they inhaled, which they would flick off with their pinky fingers. One day Daddy brought home a machine which did the rolling and sealing for them—twenty cigarettes at a time. Bonnie stood with the grown-ups, oohing and aahing as they all watched the amazing machine. "I just borrowed it," Daddy said. "I have to take it back to the boys tomorrow."

Daddy didn't smoke much, just a long drag now and then from Mama's cigarette. He took in a lot of smoke, inhaling deeply, then made smoke rings as he exhaled. He could even do this through his nose. The kids liked to watch, trying to poke their fingers through the middle, as the curls drifted upwards.

"Do it again, please, please Daddy, they begged, but he was only good for a drag or two. Aunt Lillian tried to make smoke rings, too, but it wasn't the same. Bonnie thought it was because her nose was so long and the smoke couldn't get out fast enough.

But Aunt Lillian played the piano wonderfully, and she taught Bonnie the chords at the beginning of *Tonight We Love* and how to roll the chords hand over hand, up and down the keys. Bonnie loved to hear her aunt play *Jealousy* and *Elegy* and especially *Tangerine*. Wonderful Aunt Lilian. She had a job as a secretary; she wore nice clothes and had a boyfriend, Dewey, the boss's son. She and Dewey would park in his car in front of the house until late at night. Bonnie could see the car from the upstairs bathroom window and imagined them hugging and kissing.

"Lillian, get in here!" her grandmother would yell from the front door. She had to yell several times before Lillian would get out of the car, laughing. It was the same routine in the mornings when her grandmother would try to get Lillian out of bed in time for work. "Lillaaaaane, get up now! You're late," Grandma's voice would roll upstairs through the heating grates in the floor.

She and Annie slept in the same bed with Aunt Lillian in the first upstairs bedroom. Bonnie was in the middle so it was crowded, smashed in like that. Her aunts nose breathed out soft snores onto her cheek. She longed for her friend, Rita, in Crystal Falls and wondered if she would ever see her again. She was beginning to forget what Rita looked like.

There was a large photo—a wedding photo—of Grandma and

Grandpa Smith on the wall by the foot of the bed. They were dressed in their wedding attire. Grandma wore a high stand-up ruffled collar and a pleated blouse, tied with a wide sash around her waist. Grandpa wore a black, four buttoned waist coat, narrow pants, and a skinny tie, both looked young and strait-laced.

When Bonnie looked at that photo at night, Grandma and Grandpa Smith seemed to be looking directly at her. She could just make them out from the dim light always on outside the bedroom door in the small hall on the stair landing. Lying back on her pillow, she tried to enter the picture.

It seemed to come to life, and other people from an older time began to appear in the background, moving about and dancing in a ghostly manner with one other. Bonnie felt so much a part of the scene, her body seemed to float along with the dancers. She tried to hold onto the vision, but eventually drifted off to sleep.

There were two other bedrooms upstairs, at the back of the house. The one next to Lillian's was Grandma's and the next one was for Augie and Alan. Across the hall was a fourth bedroom at the front of the house, where Daddy and Mama slept. It was the biggest room. Daddy and his brothers had slept there as boys.

The stairs curved around up from the front door. Some of them creaked; Bonnie learned to skip over the worst ones so no one would hear her going up or down. At the bottom of the stairs was a small side window. When looking through it, the outside world seemed to ebb and flow. Grandma said it was because the glass was so old that it was running back into the sand from which glass was made. She said it was sick glass.

Bonnie liked to stop there and dream about a different world that was a place like the heaven Daddy always talked about, everything was beautiful and full of wonderful things too impossible to imagine. It was for good Catholics, who could skip right over Purgatory after they died, *if* they had accumulated enough indulgences in their lifetime and were faithful to the teachings of the church. Bonnie hoped she would make it.

In the upstairs hall was a bookcase with four shelves. The books had titles like *Swiss Family Robinson, Gulliver's Travels,* and *Robinson Crusoe.* Grandma let them play library with these books; Bonnie made tags for each one, which she kept when Annie and Augie checked one out, carrying them importantly around the house a few times, then returning them so the tags could be reinserted. They were serious about this game. Alan tried to play, too, but Bonnie wouldn't let him because he was too little and she was afraid he would damage the books. Bonnie always played the part of the librarian.

She tried to read the books and could say the words, but she couldn't always understand what they were talking about. Grandma said they were "great books," so she kept trying to read them, mostly reaching the end, thinking they must be important, yet finding them tedious.

Mama gave Bonnie the job of lying down with Alan when it was his bed time, so he wouldn't be afraid. Alan seemed to be afraid of so many things. On many foggy nights as she lay next to him, the low, moaning sound of the fog horn warned ships of impending disaster. Drifting through the open bedroom window, it gave her a feeling not only of calm, but also of uncertainty as she watched the small face of her brother sink into sleep.

Chapter 14

Summers in Marquette had a teasing air. Everyone knew it wouldn't last, so grabbing onto every moment was mandated. Bonnie made two new friends, Ruth, and Charlotte. Although she didn't forget Rita, she never did write to her. But her new friendships were a bit tricky, as these two friends didn't like each other. One friend, Ruth, lived on the same street as Bonnie, and Charlotte lived a few blocks farther north in a rundown area. Bonnie's street had a sidewalk, but Charlotte's did not.

Charlotte liked to fight, kick, and hit when she was irritated. Ruth was placid, content to sit on her porch shelling garden peas or pitting cherries picked from their cherry tree. Bonnie didn't mind helping with this activity because she got to eat some of the tiny sweet green peas and the rather sour cherries.

Bonnie liked them both, but preferred Charlotte.

Charlotte was more exciting; her friends had to be on their guard lest they say the wrong thing. Her house seemed to invite secrets and lies. Her mother and father were never around, and Bonnie never went inside, sensing danger. Charlotte lied a lot, and Bonnie was becoming good at telling lies, too. When Augie accused her of saying a bad word, she always had an answer like "I didn't say 'fart,' I said 'part.' Augie said that bad word, and he's blaming me so he doesn't get spanked."

She became careful around Annie and Augie, knowing they would tattle. She stuffed so many bad words into her head, thinking one day she would spill all of them out, sometimes she unleashed them quietly in the upstairs bathroom for practice.

The bathroom became a place of discovery. She noticed her pee part was often itchy and found she could relieve the itch by gently rubbing the forbidden area. One thing she couldn't relieve was the soreness around her nipples. They seemed to be a little swollen and her blouse rubbing against the skin was a constant irritant. *I'm so miserable*, she thought. She didn't tell anyone. Ruthie had something called a training bra. Bonnie was afraid to ask her mother about getting one. Talking about body parts, given what she knew about going insane, would be impossible.

Bonnie was drawing further and further away from Mama and Daddy. If she thought of her parents at all, resentment would flare up over their strict ways, like being called in for bedtime before her friends, even if it was still daylight, or being made to take Alan in his walker in the afternoons while Mama napped. She hated when Alan would fill his diaper on these walks, she pushed his walker faster and faster on the sidewalk past her friend's house, so Ruthie wouldn't get a whiff of the smell.

Bonnie's parents seemed to always be somewhere on the fringes of her important circle of activities. She distrusted most adults, thinking them capable of betrayal. Why? Maybe because she noticed that they told lies—about what time someone came home or how much they liked someone when they really didn't like them at all. She had heard them talking of things done by others that should have been private, like someone had cancer or someone was having trouble with their marriage. Her parents were no better, especially when they were talking behind Bonnie's back.

"Bonnie's friends with that Charlotte," she heard her mother tell Daddy.

"Keep them apart, Helen. That girl's a bad influence. Charlotte's father is always drunk in the bars."

I can only do so much, Will. I've got three others to look out for." They went back and forth for a while. Bonnie got tired of listening to them argue in the kitchen. She left and walked to Ruthie's house.

Once when she had a terrible sore throat, her daddy took her to a doctor, who made her open her mouth and say "aaah," then Will held her jaw apart while the doctor took a big stick with cotton on the end, which he had dipped into a container of iodine. He pushed the swab into her forced-open mouth, painting the bitter reddish stuff all around the back of her throat. She gagged when he was done. "We had to do this, Bonnie," her dad said. "You had white pus on your tonsils."

Bonnie had heard about tonsils. Charlotte had had hers cut out. "That's a lot worse than your throat painting," Charlotte said. Charlotte always had to have something worse than Bonnie.

Another time, while crawling over a neighbor's fence to get a crab apple, she ripped open part of her knee on the barbed wire along the top of the fence. She hid the injury from her mother, knowing she wasn't supposed to go after the apples. She didn't want more iodine. She wrapped an old rag around the wound. It seemed to take forever for the bleeding to stop. She comforted herself with the thought that now she had another sin to confess. Did anyone notice her hurting? No! They were too busy with whatever had to be done to get through the day.

"Don't walk on the kitchen floor, Bonnie," her mother warned, "I've just finished waxing it."

Floors were always being washed or waxed. Coming in the front door with wet boots left a trail of dirty water.

"Don't walk in the living room with your boots on," was a common cry. Things had to be clean.

The wallpaper in the dining room was covered with smoky residue from the coal stove. It was stoked with coal carried up from the cellar in winter. Everyone was given cans of rubbery wallpaper cleaner to remove the black soot at weekly intervals. There was no end to chores that had to be done upstairs and downstairs at Grandma Smiths. Even so, the place still maintained its air of griminess. Aunt Lillian said she couldn't help with the cleaning because it would ruin her nail polish. Grandma didn't make her.

Aunt Lillian was special. She came and went as she pleased. She was the princess, always wearing new things, coating her legs with cream that mimicked silk stockings, putting Mum cream deodorant on her under arms so her blouses wouldn't stain from sweat, spraying perfume on her wrists, demanding hot water for the bathtub, which had to be carried up in kettles from the downstairs kitchen, and dancing—always dancing—around the house.

One day she placed a pattern on the living room floor and said to Bonnie, "C'mon, I'll teach you the box step." She counted to four as Bonnie moved her left foot forward, then the right opposite, then the left to the right, then the same thing over again, only now backwards. Bonnie practiced every day until it became easy. Annie learned, too. She was faster than Bonnie. The same box step turned into a jitterbug with a little variation, then the waltz. Augie and Alan refused to join in, though Alan did sort of jump up and down trying to imitate them. He was still little, only four.

Aunt Lillian always told tales about the nightclubs she went to with her girlfriends. If she went to a movie, she would tell them the whole plot, thrilling Bonnie with the love stories. Her favorite story was from a movie called *Random Harvest*. The terrible amnesia and the beautiful garden path at the end of the movie where the two lovers finally got together entranced Bonnie. She wanted Aunt Lillian's world, which seemed to be the same world as the movie stories she recounted.

One time she took Bonnie to the movie theater. They had to pay because Uncle Gordon didn't own this one. The movie playing was *The Wizard of Oz*. The magical part for Bonnie was when the house landed in Munchkin Land and Dorothy opened the farmhouse door, revealing a scene of brilliant color. It was overwhelming. Aunt Melanie said it was Technicolor. She never forgot this feeling of wonder, longing for her own world to be something other than sepia.

After the movie, they walked downhill. Every road in Marquette was steep—either up or down. They walked to the Bon Ton café for an ice cream sundae. Bonnie tried to reconcile sundae with Sunday. One was so delicious and the other was a way of getting to heaven, where they maybe had sundaes. Daddy had often told them the story of the candy house in the woods. In that story Bonnie, Annie, Augie, and Alan took a walk through a forest, got lost, and found a house made of candy, that they ate to their hearts' content, Daddy finally found them, tied the house to his car, and brought the whole scene home to Mama, who planted the house in the back garden, and every time they were good, they could break off a piece of the candy and eat it. After seeing the *Wizard of Oz* movie, Bonnie imagined this story in Technicolor.

Aunt Lillian was her sponsor for Confirmation, and she gave Bonnie a white holy missal with colored ribbons hanging from the spine, which had to be moved to the appropriate page for each Sunday and Holy Day. The pages were thin, and when the book was closed it looked like the pages between the covers were painted with gold. On one page of the book—on the left side—were the Latin words said by the priest and the altar boys, *Kyrie, Confiteor Deo Omnipotente, Gloria, Credo In Unum Deo, Sanctus, and Agnus Dei.* Opposite, on the right side, were the English translations. Bonnie loved this book, loved sitting in the pew moving the colored ribbons from page to page, her eyes jumping from the left to the right side of the pages, not minding being in church at all. The elastic on her hat still hurt her neck, though, and the wooden kneelers dug into her skinny knee bones. Some people leaned back on their seats while kneeling, but not Bonnie. "Kneel up straight, Bonnie," her father would command in a quiet whisper.

Chapter 15

The cathedral was across the street from the Bishop Baraga Catholic School. This was where Bonnie was to attend fourth grade. She wasn't happy about going back to Catholic school. The walk from her Grandma's house to the school was long. From the far north side of Marquette, Bonnie had to go up and down many hills, past the downtown area, across railroad tracks, under a bridge, finally reaching the looming grey stone school building.

Every day there was a new catechism answer to memorize, and she went over the words many times on the walk with Charlotte. Bonnie wanted to go to Graveret, the public school where Ruthie went. Daddy would *not* allow it. He told Grandma that the children had been poisoned enough in the Crystal Falls school system. Bonnie couldn't see how. She'd loved her teachers, especially Mrs. Bean, and she'd felt like a smart person there.

Now the day began again with "Good morning Sister," and a feeling of dread, wondering if she would be called on to stand and recite the answer to the catechism question. Mornings dragged on. She was always hungry, though her mother had made sure there was plenty of cocoa and toast for breakfast, followed by a big spoon of cod liver oil. Ruthie took her oil in a capsule, but the capsules weren't in their food budget.

"Open up, Bonnie," said Mother, "Here's your oil." It tasted so awful. Bonnie's tongue and throat were coated with the stuff, and she gagged when it went down with a shudder.

"Why do I have to take this stuff?" she asked.

"So you don't get sick," said mother.

"This makes me sick, Mama." Mama ignored her comment.

At school, the noon bell finally rang. All the children were marched down to the basement where they had lunch. Bonnie had a white bread and butter lettuce sandwich from home and the school cook gave her a bowl of warm cabbage soup. She liked the soup. Some of the kids had lunch buckets with pictures on them. They contained fruit and bologna sandwiches. Bonnie carried her sandwich in a paper bag. She so wanted a lunch bucket. *Why can't I have one like the other* kids? She wondered.

Once she saw one sitting empty on one of the long metal lunch tables. There was no one nearby, so she took it, again feeling the thrill of the hidden act. She told Mama, "Charlotte gave it to me. It was her old one and she didn't use any more." Putting her name on it with green crayon— green being her favorite color—she thought of the seventh commandment, "Thou shalt not steal." Now she was again a liar as well as a thief. Her penance at confession the next Saturday was a whole rosary. "You must give the bucket back as well," commanded the priest, but she didn't. The rosary was enough, she thought. In Crystal Falls she only got three Our Fathers and three Hail Marys.

Salvation was still attainable. On All Soul's Day, the class was lined up before the heavy cathedral doors. Going inside, they were instructed to recite an Our Father, Hail Mary, and a Glory Be to the Father. This would release a soul from purgatory. They had an hour to do this exercise, going in and out as many times as they could.

The scene was one of children running in, kneeling, racing through the prayers, racing outside, running in again, over and over, eager to get as many souls as they could out of the burning purgatory, which wasn't quite as hot as hell, but still a painful place. Bonnie only knew one person who died, her grandfather, so she included her own soul in most of the prayers. Anyway, everyone said Grandpa Smith had gone straight to heaven because of the host leaping into his mouth from the hands of the priest. She thought of the prayers as insurance for future sins, in case some of them turned out to be mortal.

Bonnie still liked the singing class best. Her favorite song from the blue music book was *On Top of Old Smoky*. On Saturdays at the

WMAQ radio station, kids could sign up to sing or recite something into the microphone. Bonnie always signed up, and one Saturday she was finally called for a turn.

Daddy was there, too, with his band during the same one o'clock hour. They paid him and his band, because union rules said radio stations could only play live music. Daddy had two jobs, the Piqua factory and his playing gigs. He liked playing more than anything.

Bonnie was nervous, not liking her latest hair cut that showed off her one big ear. But she sang as well as she could. After Bonnie sang her "Old Smoky" the announcer said, "This little girl has a great future." Her dad gave her a big smile. She kept her white tasseled beanie on the whole while, trying to contain her ear.

Walking home after school was rather fun if it wasn't too cold. Running along the curb in the downhill places there was a steady stream of melting snow water where she and Charlotte floated sticks and butterfly seeds that twirled down from the maple trees, watching to see how far they would go before being drawn into a sewer pipe. Sometimes they split the seed. The inside of the seed was sticky. It looked funny when they stuck it onto their noses. The girls laughed at each other until the seeds fell off.

The cold made the walk seem longer because of the heavy clothing. Snow began right after Halloween that year. Bonnie was made to wear long underwear, folded over at the ankles so that the long brown, ribbed cotton stockings held up with elastic garters could go over them. Next came the snow pants with suspenders, goulashes, and a jacket, all from a used clothing place. Mama tied crocheted strings to her mittens, which were inserted into the sleeves of the jacket so they wouldn't get lost.

Bonnie's white crocheted hat with a large tassel, came from her Grandma Johnson. Once she even sent an orange, wool, button down sweater, but it was so scratchy on her skin that Bonnie refused to wear it. Mama made a lining for it from some cotton fabric. Then it was all right. Her mother was good at sewing.

There was a record snow fall that year. Daddy heard on the radio that the downtown was burning and the fire engines couldn't get through to the scene. Most of the town was razed by the flames. Snow drifts were at an all- time high. Schools were closed for several days, to the delight of the children.

The local ice rink was crowded, especially at night, which was Bonnie's favorite time to be there. She wore Aunt Lillian's old black skates, laces tightened just so, and circled the perimeter of the icy area, trying to keep her ankles from collapsing, often falling. The rink was lighted by a single dim light post at night. The boys made a game of turning it off periodically, when a boy was near a girl he wanted to kiss. Once during this moment of darkness, Bonnie felt a quick, cold brush of lips against her cheeks. Had she imagined it? Ruthie said it was Billy Marlow and gave Bonnie a knowing smile.

All the girls liked Billy. He had dark curly hair and big brown eyes. Bonnie felt all tingly after the kiss, hoping for some further contact with Billy, but all the boys were huddled together near the lighting post, laughing loudly, making Bonnie feel like the butt of some joke. She told Ruthie she hated boys but she secretly didn't.

She liked another boy, Benny Norman, who lived around the corner from her Grandma's house. He was known for telling stories—lies mostly—about how strong he was, how fast he could climb trees, and how much money he had. He was cute, too, in a more sharp, pointy way, skinny bodied, a smirky a know it-all look on his face.

He lived with his grandpa and grandma. His mother had left him there one day when he was little and had taken off with some fellow who worked at the tavern on the corner of the next street. Benny's father had run off too, shortly before he was born. Benny was always hanging around Bonnie, but he didn't try to kiss her or anything.

Benny's grandpa was scary, but not at first. When Bonnie had gone to Benny's house during the past summer to see if he was at home, his grandpa was sitting in the back yard. "Benny's not here," he said. "He'll be back in a little while. He went to pick up something for Grandma." He called Bonnie to come over and wait while he told her a story.

Liking stories, she came and sat hesitantly on his knee. Suddenly she felt his hand moving on her leg, up toward her underpants. She pulled away and ran for her own house. She became afraid of the old man after that. She didn't tell anyone, not even the priest in confession, not knowing how to say what had happened, though she knew it was wrong. *Whose sin is it? Mine? The old man's?* The sin business was complicated.

Chapter 16

In January, Annie and Bonnie were stricken with a rash, sore throat, and vomiting. Scarlet fever was again making its rounds, and the doctor was called. Yes, they had it.

"But Annie had scarlet fever once before. "How can this be?" asked her mother who feared a quarantine.

"It's been known to happen a second time," the doctor propounded, putting his stethoscope back into his black bag. "It's definitely scarlet fever; however, the county no longer operates a pest house. They will be admitted to the contagious ward at St. Luke's Hospital." This was welcome news. The quarantine sign on the house would only be posted for seven days, instead of the previous twenty-one they had endured the last time.

Bonnie and Annie had never been inside a hospital, but it wasn't far from their house. Strange room, strange beds. The room seemed so big. They were there for twenty-one days, pampered by nurses who let them help make their own beds, showing them how to do the proper tucks around the edges, even setting up a small table where they could play board games. Bonnie lorded it over Annie, scaring her with ghost stories at night, sometimes scaring herself in the process.

When the nurses weren't around, they often jumped up and down on the beds, trying to see who could jump the highest. Bonnie didn't feel sick at all after the first few days. Her parents came to visit a few times, standing at the far end of the long, wide hall outside their room. Bonnie and Annie waved to them from their doorway, not being too loud, as other sick people on the ward didn't want to hear any noise.

"Nurse, do something about those girls in the next room," complained a man in the next room who had the mumps. "I can't get any rest with all the racket."

Others complained, too. The nurse told Bonnie and Annie to always keep their door shut.

I want to stay here forever, Bonnie thought, but Annie often cried for Mama. Annie was certainly Mama's favorite, next to Alan.

Finally, the day came for departure. Arriving back at Grandma Smith's house was a shock. Everything seemed so small, compared to the enormous hospital room—the low ceiling, the narrow hall to the kitchen, the dark stairway with the wooden steps. She stood in the kitchen feeling disoriented, trying to make her body adjust to her surroundings.

"Hi, Bonnie," Augie said. "Are you going to stay here now?"

"I guess so," she answered. She felt like a stranger. She longed for the hospital.

The hospital was within walking distance and she took Charlotte there to show her around. One could enter through a seldom-used side door and get right to the elevator area. The elevator was fun. They got inside, pushed buttons, and rode up and down many times. Other people got on, but they just stood back against the wall, being quiet, pretending to be invisible. Maybe they were, because no one ever asked what they were doing there.

Across from the hospital was the Normal School, where Aunt Tilly had gone to become a teacher. The hill behind the school was steep and wooded, another place to play in winter. Kids took pieces of cardboard and sat on them, sliding down fast over the snow, laughing as they fell in a pile at the bottom. The boys and girls made it a point to get tangled up. Bonnie always tried to wind up with Billy Marlow if Benny wasn't there.

In late spring, when there were only small patches of snow, Bonnie liked to go off by herself into those same woods, poking on the forest floor through the dead wet leaves with a stick, looking for wildflowers—jack-in-the-pulpits, lady slippers and purple violets. She was fascinated by their names. She pretended they were real people, trapped in flower shapes, and she never picked them, fearing they would die.

She did pick clover, though. There was so much of it in the open areas. She and Annie liked to braid the clover into wreaths for crowns on their heads and play princess games, wearing Mother's dresses and high heels. They tried to make clover perfume by stuffing the flower heads into small jars of water, covering the jars, and checking every day to see if there was a good smell coming from the mixture. That wasn't a success, just a yucky, moldy, bad smelling mess.

Spring smells were good, especially the lilacs with their lush fragrance. Some shrubs had small white berries which popped when they were stepped on. The bleeding-heart bushes were amazing, their bending branches heavy with heart-shaped flowers, little blackish strings falling from each heart like dark blood.

With the snow nearly gone the walk to school was easier, free from smothering outer garments. The May Crowning was coming soon, Sister announced one morning. One of the girls in her class would be chosen to put a crown of flowers on the statue of the Virgin Mary. This happened every May first, but this was the first time Bonnie was old enough to take part in the ceremony. Bonnie wanted to wear the white dress and blue cape and gold crown and carry the flower crown through the double line of the other girls.

"Charlotte, do you think they'll pick one of us?" Bonnie asked as they were walking home from school one day.

"Not likely me," said Charlotte. "I never get the answer right to the catechism questions."

"Well, I only missed once or twice," said Bonnie." I so want to be chosen."

Charlotte gave her a playful push and they both fell onto the curb where they sat laughing.

Bonnie didn't want to be in the queen's court where the girls held hands forming a bridge under which the queen processed. They only wore a blue cape, no white veil. Every night, Bonnie prayed— always on her knees— that she would be chosen. Neither she nor Charlotte were picked. Aunt Lillian said it was always a girl with rich parents from the French Catholic Church downtown who would be given the honor.

I want to be rich, I will be rich, Bonnie thought. *If you're rich, your prayers are answered. You must be rich.* She had a goal. She wondered where rich people lived. *Not in this area,* she thought. *Everything around here is so drab. Our family is stuck here on the northside.*

The north side of Marquette had a three-block area populated by Finnish people. They kept to themselves. Bonnie walked through this area when she and Charlotte headed for a swim. On the way to Fortune Lake they passed an old burned out house. They liked to sneak into this building and poke around the papers and other bits of trash lying on the floor. There were the remains of a piano, strings exposed on the metal harp-shaped backboard, standing on its end. Running their hands across the strings would make an eerie sound which echoed throughout the blackened house. Then they would run out, screaming, scared witless and continue the way to the lake.

Once walking through the Finnish area alone, Bonnie saw a little boy standing outside one of the houses. He was wearing a striped knitted cap of many colors, snuggly covering the back of his head as though it was part of his hair. He stared at her as she passed by. He seemed strange.

Her Aunt Lillian told her the Finns had different practices, even able to work magic spells which would paralyze anyone who looked too long at them. "Hurry quickly by," she had warned. "Keep your eyes straight ahead." Bonnie thought this odd, but obeyed her aunt, half believing her, half wanting to stare and see what it was like to be under a spell like the wildflowers. She thought of the freezing game where the 'it' person called "Freeze" at a certain point— no one knew when, and the kids who were running about a circle in silly poses had to freeze. Whoever moved from that position became the next 'it'. Hardly the spell Bonnie wished for.

On the last day of fourth grade she was given a passing certificate to the fifth grade, which she wasn't looking forward to, because the fifth-grade nun was rumored to be extra hard. The sixth graders to be warned that the nun was mean. Bonnie noticed that Daddy hadn't been around for a few days. She rarely thought about her parents, avoiding contact as much as possible. "Where's Daddy?" she asked Aunt Lillian.

"He's got a new job at a glider plant in Copper Ridge," Lillian said. "It's good money. He's there now looking for a place for your family to live."

"Where's Copper Ridge?" Bonnie asked, "Is it far?"

"Far," her aunt said, "about a hundred miles from here, but the moncy is good."

She ran to find her mother who was in the kitchen, crying.

"Mama, is it true? "Are we moving again?"

Her mother looked helplessly at Bonnie and didn't answer. Bonnie knew it was true.

Another move, she thought, *but the money is good. Maybe this means we'll be rich at last.*

Copper Ridge, Michigan
1940

Chapter 17

How did this happen, thought Bonnie? Daddy's new job still did not make the Smith family rich, but somehow Bonnie felt immediately at home in this interesting place. She grew to love it, and for the next several years it was her haven from which she set out on exploring expeditions throughout the entire building, up and down their street—Margaret Street—and all points beyond.

A picture of Bonnie, Annie, Augie and Alan reveals a step ladder of kids, wearing clothes looking too big, standing outside at the bottom of five cement steps, with metal railings, leading up to twenty-one wooden steps. They are all squinting as they look directly into the sun. To the left of the steps was another set of cement steps, wider, leading into double doors. There is a sign above this door. It reads: THE CITY BAKERY.

A wide window to the right of the bakery door displayed a machine that picked up dough, squeezed it through a hole, pushed it out, forming a small disc with a center hole. The machine then plopped the disc into a container of hot oil, where it remained as it expanded— not very long—then got picked up by the machine arm, turned over and plopped again into another pot of hot oil.

Bonnie liked to watch this process. This was her house, or part of it anyway, and the doughnut aroma filled the whole building. At the top of the wooden stairs was a long, rather rickety wooden porch and two apartments, one of which was always empty. The second door on the left was for the Smiths. The first door was theirs, too, but it was never used, except when Daddy and a friend maneuvered the upright Howard piano up the twenty-six steps and into the front room. The piano came from Grandma Johnson. She also gave Mama her sewing machine, the kind with a foot treadle that had to be pumped up and down for the needle to move as the cloth was pushed under the area where stitches were laid out in a neat row along the seams of the garments Mama made for the children. The sewing machine was in one of the small bedrooms.

"This is where you and Annie will sleep," said Mama. "Look it has a window."

"It's nice window, Mama, bigger than the window in Aunt Lillian's bedroom," said Bonnie. "Look Annie, we can see right out onto the street from up here." She put her arm around Annie as she said this, moving her to the window to look out.

"There's a truck on the street, Bonnie, parked right below our window," said Annie.

"That's a bakery truck, Annie. There's a bakery right below us. We'll have lots of treats, you'll see. Doughnuts. Yum!"

Annie who had been a bit teary eyed, was mollified by that.

Bonnie quickly committed all the rooms to memory. There was a front room, kitchen, two bedrooms, a tiny hall between the kitchen, a living room, and one small closet. There was a large bathroom off the kitchen with tub, sink, medicine cabinet and toilet stool. Alongside the sink was a shelf, which held Daddy's shaving cup and razor. Behind the door of the bathroom was a hook which held Daddy's razor strop.

Mama and Daddy slept in the second bedroom that had a door connected to Bonnie's room. Augie and Alan were put to sleep in Mama's bed and, when she and Daddy retired, the boys were moved to an open-out couch in the front room for the rest of the night.

This must be all right, thought Bonnie. *We've moved such a long way from Marquette. There's no Grandma Smith or Grandma Johnson to help.* Bonnie hoped Daddy would keep his new job. Her memory of the years in Marquette seemed dreamlike, moving about from shack to shack, bunking in with her grandmas, life tossing and turning each time Daddy lost his job, but now their family was safe and together in this space above a bakery, looking out on roads and tree tops and the roofs of houses beneath. She believed she would survive and that being rich was still in the cards.

Chapter 18

Mama didn't always go with Daddy on his frequent gigs, so when she went to bed, her reading light shone into Bonnie's bedroom. Her cigarette smoke wafted in, too, and it was comforting to know that she was settled in and not scurrying about looking for dust or dirt.

Bonnie had started referring to her parents—in her head, but never aloud—by this or that name. They seemed to be different people at different times. *Daddy,* for instance, was the loving guy who took the kids on walking treks up the local hills looking for berries. He was also the man who, when coming home late at night after a gig, would come into their bedroom saying, "Good night, lover," while making sure the girls were warmly covered.

Will was the fun guy playing the piano or banjo, doing magic tricks, hosting other musicians for late night jam sessions, wearing a stocking cap made from Mama's old nylons to keep his hair slicked back when he napped, making him look so comical.

Father was the one to be afraid of. He often used the strop on Bonnie's brothers, and sometimes on Bonnie herself when Mama complained to him about the quarreling and noisiness, saying it gave her a headache. *Father* was the one who looked out for the children's morals, making sure everyone knelt together in the living room after supper for the family rosary, praying that Mama would start to attend church. Mama stayed in the kitchen.

"Church and praying isn't in my catalogue of chores," Bonnie heard her tell Daddy.

Father was the guy who blew his temper if one of his tools went missing or was out of place in his tool drawer. "Oh shit!" he would bellow when this happened. "Where's my screwdriver?"

In Mama's case, *Helen* was the woman who liked to have fun. Helen was always playing card games, drinking her quart of beer every evening, going with the neighbor to bingo games, telling her children stories of her growing up in Negaunee, singing in her tuneless voice little Swedish songs, like "Kum Letle Flicka," while dancing about with Alan in her arms, her loose house dress flaring out.

Mama made them egg sandwiches with catsup when Bonnie were hungry at night, let Bonnie use the meat grinder for making potato sausage, made a game of who was to have the largest pudding in the pudding glasses lined up on the kitchen counter. The puddings were all the same, but the kids imagined one was the fullest by that almost imperceptible fraction.

"This one's mine," Bonnie would announce, taking the pudding dish and hiding it in a kitchen cabinet behind the cups.

"Why do you always get the biggest one, Bonnie?" asked Annie.

"Because I'm the oldest, that's why, Annie. Get used to it."

Yet the puddings all measured the same to the discerning eye. Bonnie's statement was more of an assertion of her place in the family.

"Please stop the arguing. They're all the same," said Mama, trying to settle the matter.

Mama had all but disappeared since the move to Copper Ridge. There wasn't time for hugs or kisses. *Mama* only emerged for Bonnie in Copper Ridge, when she let Bonnie read her copy of *Gone With the Wind*. *Mama* was also there when she didn't tell Daddy things such as Bonnie's habit of smearing on lipstick after leaving the house for school.

Mother was the woman who would chase the boys—and sometimes Bonnie—around the small apartment waving a butcher knife, cursing, screaming, threatening to do them in. She was still beautiful, even at those times, with her face twisted up and her eyes popping out, looking so scary.

"I'll get you, you little sons of bitches, stop!" she would yell during the chase.

Usually Augie was the culprit, but when it was Bonnie, it was the worst. Bonnie tried to look the same scary way when she was left to baby sit for Augie and Alan, who were the meanest teasers and who would laugh wildly at her, making her even madder. Her notion of being in command was short lived.

"Get to bed right now, Alan, Mama said you have to mind me," Bonnie would plead, as her brother laughed and kept jumping up and down on the mattress. She would end up hitting him so hard but he still refused to mind her. Augie was the same way. She felt so frustrated by their behavior that she ended up screaming just like her mother.

The place was small, but Mama didn't complain much.

"The rent is only eighteen dollars a month, Helen," Bonnie heard Daddy explain to Mama as Bonnie was drying the dishes from supper. "It's the best I could find. A lot of people are moving to Copper Ridge because of the glider plant."

"But, a kerosene stove, Will, it's hard to cook on a kerosene stove!" Mama cried.

The kerosene stove with two burners stood on one wall of the kitchen and on the floor beside it was a black metal oven. The oven had to be placed on the burners when Mama was baking. Once, after the baking was finished and the hot oven was moved to the floor, Augie sat on it and burned his bum. He cried and cried. Mama spread some of her zinc ointment on his bottom. She used this salve for every kind of injury.

The kerosene bottle attached to the stove had another use besides lighting the burners. Whenever the children had a bad cold and couldn't stop coughing at night, they were given a teaspoon of the kerosene. Bonnie hated this because the taste was so bad, and after swallowing it she felt like she couldn't breathe; however, the coughing did stop. The worst salve was *Musterole,* which was spread over her chest and throat, then a coarse cloth was tightly wrapped around the same area, burning the cold right out of her. That usually worked, too.

The kitchen floor was covered with thin linoleum. Mother scrubbed it on her hands and knees every night after supper. She hated dirt. In summer flies came in every time the screen door was opened They liked to land in a drowsy stupor on the kitchen ceiling. Sometimes they were caught on sticky, curling fly paper hanging from the overhead light, or even better, trapped by Daddy. He would climb on a chair with a glass of water that he placed slowly over each stupefied fly until they fell into the water glass and drowned.

"Careful, Will, don't fall, cautioned Mama. You'll get water all over the floor. I'm too tired to scrub it again.

"Don't worry, Helen, just hold the chair steady," Daddy would say.

The fly trapping was a nightly ritual in summer. After the dreaded family rosary was finished, Bonnie liked to watch the flies drop in the water and drown. She didn't see what good the rosary did about getting Mama to church.

Mama liked to keep things organized. She had a place for every little thing and knew exactly where everything belonged. "Your pajamas are in your drawer, Bonnie. You know that. Get ready for bed right now," she would say in her mad voice.

Annie and Bonnie had a bureau chest in their room. They each had a drawer. Bonnie's was the top one, Annie's the second, and the two bottom drawers were for Augie and Alan. They were never supposed to go into one another's drawers. That was a rule. Bonnie always broke the rule, wanting to know if there was something hidden. Some forbidden thing, like cigarettes or candy.

Mama and Daddy had a dresser with a mirror in their room that Bonnie liked to finger into when she had the chance. The top drawer held Mama's bits of costume jewelry and her good engagement necklace. On the dresser were two pictures, one of Mama's family from before she was married and one of Mama and Daddy in their engagement picture. The before picture showed Grandma and Grandpa Johnson and Mama and her brother, Lemmy, all looking much younger. Mama had a cute bob haircut and Lemmy had a bowl haircut. Grandma had black horn-rimmed glasses and Grandpa looked quite handsome, still having hair. Lemmy looked a lot like Grandpa Johnson. In the other drawers were Daddy's work shirts and Mama's dresses—house dresses they were called—neatly folded.

Under the dresses, Bonnie often found magazines with names like *Redbook* and *Ladies Home Journal*. She wasn't supposed to read these, as Daddy had forbidden such trash. He didn't want Mama reading them either, but she did and so did Bonnie. She was quick about putting them aside if Daddy came around. Sometimes Bonnie heard her parents argue about it—not loudly, but in strident whispers.

She could make out stuff like "Keep them away from the kids, Helen, especially Bonnie, she's getting bigger." Sometimes Mama cried, then Daddy would hug her until she stopped. Bonnie liked to watch them embrace, Mama in her silk underslip, Daddy always fully clothed. She never saw him without his shirt and trousers except one time when he forgot to lock the bathroom door, and she saw him standing there peeing, his pants dropped about his ankles. She backed out quickly before he saw her. He seemed so ordinary, like her brothers, whom she had watched when they were playing the pee game with their friends to see who could piss the farthest with their stream. She felt jealous, because she couldn't join in. She would search around her own parts 'down there' while in the bathroom alone, trying to figure out where everything was. The bathroom was still a favorite room.

There was another chest of drawers was in that room. That was the biggest one. It held mostly towels and linens. Next to this chest was the wringer washing machine. Every wash day—which was usually Monday—before everyone was up, Mama wheeled the washer into the kitchen, next to the kerosene stove, where she had a boiler of water heating. She transferred water from the boiler with a long-handled pot into the washer. She then cut a bar of strong *Fels Naphtha* soap into the water and plugged the machine into the only electrical outlet, which started the water to swoosh and the swooshing made the soap chips dissolve.

The dirty clothes were piled into the whirling water, swished around for several minutes, then lifted out one by one and put through a revolving wringer. The wet clothes then fell into a clothes basket beneath the wringer that Mama carried down the twenty-six steps to a clothes line strung between two trees. They were left to flap in the wind until they were dry.

In winter the clothes froze on the line, so she carried the icy clothes back up the twenty-six steps into the house and draped them over the steam radiators like ghostly white tents where they would finish drying. The drying clothes made the room smell fresh, the outside coming in.

Bonnie felt sorry for her mama when she watched her struggle with the washing. She feared her mother's legs would give out, especially when she was climbing up and down the stairs with the heavy basket of wet or icy clothes.

I don't want to have this kind of life, thought Bonnie. *I'm going to be rich and get us all out of this life of hard labor.* She had no plan, but she was determined. *We have so little.* She thought of the one closet. It was off the living room behind a door that didn't quite close. It had only a dim, bare light bulb on the ceiling, screwed directly into the socket from which a long string fell. A small sort of flower-shaped brass piece was attached to the end of the string. Pulling the little flower turned on the light.

The closet was perfectly arranged according to the needs of each family member. Mama's two good dresses hung on a rod to the right. Everything else hung on hangers extending from hooks on the wall. Daddy had his own rod on the opposite far end, though far was an exaggeration. It was only about three steps from one end of the closet to the other. The ironing board was also stored in this space.

A small shelf that Daddy had put up above the hanging area held boxes of important papers–birth certificates, baptismal certificates, records of bills that had been paid, bills still to be paid, and letters from Grandma Johnson. She wrote weekly, usually enclosing ration stamps for sugar, meat, and flour. Bonnie knew Grandma really did worry about all of them.

"Are we ever going to see Grandma Johnson again, Mama?" asked Bonnie as she was hauling the ironing board to the kitchen. She has such a nice house. I love it there."

"Maybe someday, Bonnie," said Mama. "Negaunee is a long way off. If we had the money, maybe we could make the trip. I'd like to see my mother, too, you know. Now bring me that spray bottle from the sink, please. These clothes are too dry. I'll have to sprinkle them down."

Maybe, always maybe, thought Bonnie. She watched her mother work on the ironing, occasionally stopping for a drag on her cigarette.

"Here, Bonnie. Take this shirt and hang it on your father's side of the closet. He needs to look sharp for tonight's gig." Without looking at Bonnie, she handed her the shirt and grabbed another wrinkled blouse from the basket. Bonnie carried the white shirt to the closet. *Maybe I shouldn't have asked the question*, she thought.

Whatever space remained on the floor of the closet was for shoes and Will's melaphone, trumpet, and banjo case. That sounds crowded, but everyone knew where everything was; anyway, no one had that much.

Chapter 19

The neighborhood was made up of mostly Italian families, not all of them English-speaking. It was common gossip that many of the men had served time in the local jail for bootlegging during the thirties, coming out with a bit of money stashed away.

The houses had wooden porches and small front yards, and they were built close together. The lots were long and narrow. Behind each house was a garden. Bonnie could get into these gardens from the alley that ran behind the houses. She liked to pick a tomato, or green bean or pull a radish or carrot to eat just for the fun of it. She wasn't supposed to. She put it on her list of sins for confession.

It was a short block, but Margaret Street extended much farther east, all the way to Lake Wakesha. Bonnie's explorations from the bakery covered this block first. Next door in a nice brick house, with the best backyard garden, tended to by the old grandfather, lived the Brunos. They didn't acknowledge anyone else in the neighborhood.

There was the husband, fat and important looking, and the wife, slender, always put together, and their car, parked on their drive, a shiny car, new every two years. Mr. Bruno ran a car dealership, the only one in Copper Ridge.

"Look, Annie, the Bruno's probably have a lot of money," said Bonnie in a bragging know-it-all voice. She wanted to impress Annie. "I bet they bootlegged, too." She wasn't sure what bootlegging was, but knew it was some sort of sin.

"I think the grandfather went to jail. Watch out for him," she said, as she led Annie about the neighborhood. "He yells at everyone to keep out of his garden."

Next to them were the Columbos. Mrs. Columbo, according to their pale-faced daughter, Barbara, suffered from asthma and "would probably die from it one of these days," Barbara told Bonnie. Barbara's dad lived there, too, somewhere in the deep back of the house. He never came out, but Mrs. Columbo often sat on their tiny front porch. The house looked like it was about to fall over, the front screen door, hanging on one hinge and the small window next to it was partly covered with cardboard. "Barbara's about your age, Annie. She might be a friend for you."

"I don't think I like her, Bonnie. I tried to talk to her one day but she didn't say anything, and her face is so white. I'm afraid of her." I like the boy who lives next to her," said Annie.

"I know who you mean, Annie. Petey Hansen. I don't know what there is to like about him, except that he's short, like you."

Petey lived next door to the Columbos with his mother and grandmother, Mrs. Balducci. She had heard her mother say to Daddy that Mr. Hansen, Petey's dad, had left one day and never returned, leaving no address where he might be found. This desertion shattered Mrs. Hansen. She was a pretty lady, thin, always seen wearing a dark, greyish dress. She sat by the grandmother on their front porch swing, their heads covered with black scarves, both holding rosary beads in their hands, making whispered comments to each other when someone walked by.

Petey didn't say much, either. He wasn't very tall for ten years old, and he had a BB gun which he would point at whoever passed in front of the house, and make a loud bang with his voice. He never pulled the trigger, except once on the Fourth of July, but he didn't hit anyone.

"Gotcha, girl, bang," he would yell as Bonnie walked by, sticking her tongue out at his pathetic show of bravery.

On the east corner of the street was Tramontine's store. "No one ever goes in that store and you shouldn't either," she warned Annie. "I've been down this block before, and I went in once to see what they were selling. There was almost nothing on the shelves and the store keeper asked me to get out. He must have thought I was going to steal something. I heard someone say things other than groceries are sold there. Then there's the four women who live above the store. I've never actually seen them but I heard Mama talk about them. She says they're not nice."

"Okay, Bonnie. Let's walk on the other side of the street," said Annie in a scared voice. Bonnie loved to scare Annie.

Across the street from the Tramontine store was a large vacant lot filled mostly with weeds, the prickly kind, which stuck to their anklets whenever they cut across. Everyone cut across this lot. There were only three other houses on the opposite side of the street, facing the bakery.

Right across lived Mrs. Carla Romongnoli. She had a beauty shop on her enclosed front porch. Bonnie got a permanent wave there more than once, the kind where her hair was rolled on metal rollers hanging from cords which were attached to a metal dome above. A switch turned on the heat which ran through the cords onto the rollers, cooking curls into her hair. The cost was ten dollars. Carla—everyone called her Carla, even the kids—kept a rack of laundry hanging before the front window, waiting to be ironed. Bonnie found this odd.

She had one son, Bobby. He was fat and mean. Augie and Alan were afraid of him. Bonnie didn't like him either, but for a different reason. He liked to hide behind a corner of the bakery and pull out his wiener, pointing it at Annie and Bonnie, before quickly ducking behind the building so he wouldn't get caught. This disgusted Bonnie, but she didn't tell anyone, nor did Annie. Bobby and Bonnie were in the same grade at school. Carla said he was hard to manage. Her husband worked in the oil fields in Saudi Arabia and only came home every six months for a two-week visit.

Next to them were the Marconis. Their house, a grey stucco, was shaded by tall elms. They had one son, Raymond, who was sort of nice, but quiet. He didn't play in the street games which the neighborhood kids all liked to do on warm evenings, the favorite being Kick the Can.

"I can kick farther than you, Augie," bragged Bonnie. She was a good kicker.

"The farther you kick, the more time we have to hide, Bonnie, you dope," he yelled as he ran with Bobbie, Annie, Alan, and the boys from another block further east.

"How come you don't play with us, Raymond?" Bonnie asked him one day when she saw him on his porch swing.

"My dad has a disease which is gradually turning him to stone. When the stone reaches his lungs, he'll die. That's why," he said sadly as he swung harder and harder. "I have to help my ma get my dad ready for bed. She can't manage by herself."

Bonnie never saw Mr. Marconi, though she wanted to, and could only imagine a man made of stone. What kind of stone was it? Was it grey? Did it have tiny holes in it, like some of the rocks found on the beach? She felt sorry for Raymond.

"He was in the army, Bonnie," he's going to have a flag on his coffin, and Ma's going to get the flag, all rolled up," Raymond added a little defiantly.

Mama said there was a war still going on across the ocean and President Roosevelt wanted gliders built so soldiers and supplies could get to the troubled places. "I have to be careful with our supplies, Bonnie," she said when Bonnie asked for more butter on her sandwich. "Grocery shopping's a challenge. Sometimes I run out of flour before the end of the month. You kids had better stop complaining." Each family was mailed a precious book of ration stamps every month, for stuff in short supply because of the war. *Just about every kind of the really good food*, Bonnie thought. Grandma Johnson's extra ration books came in handy.

"Look, Will," said Mama. "Ration stamps from my mother. She and my dad can't use them all. It's just the two of them, she says in her letter. Now we'll have extra flour and sugar."

Wonderful Grandma Johnson, thought Bonnie as she watched her mother count out the stamps. Grandma hadn't forgotten them. Mama said It didn't matter if you were a big family like the Smiths, or there was just one person to a household. This made no sense to Bonnie. The Cavianis always seemed to have enough.

The Cavianis—Della and Frank—had two sons, Don and Franny

Their house was not technically on Margaret Street, because their front door faced another way. During the evening games in summer, Don, the oldest, always followed Bonnie when it was time to hide. Don liked to lie on the ground, look up Bonnie's skirt, and reach up trying to touch her underpants.

"I see London, I see France, I see someone's underpants" he would singsong under his voice.

"You're being nasty, Don. I'm going to tell your mother," she would reply with a giggle. Of course, Bonnie didn't tell. She didn't mind. She even let him touch her underpants on occasion, liking it, because he was so good looking—the handsomest boy in the neighborhood—*and* he played the accordion. *Was it a sin?* she wondered. *It's so much fun, it had to be okay.*

Chapter 20

The Smith's had a newspaper delivered daily. The carrier stuck it on top of the black mail box attached to the wall at the bottom of the wooden stairs. Bonnie's favorite part of the paper was the funnies, especially *Brenda Star* and *Lil Abner*. Daddy always took the paper first, looking over the comics, cutting out pictures of *Daisy Mae* because her skimpy outfit revealed too much of her anatomy. Sometimes Bonnie managed to glimpse the edited parts, when she volunteered to get the paper from the bottom of the wooden stairs. She walked up slowly, quickly paging through until she found the forbidden fruit. Bonnie's own little fruits, that had been so tender, were now bigger buds and were no longer painful.

The school was a nice surprise. Two schools actually, across from one another and the shared the same tarred play area. Augie, who was in second grade, and Alan, now in kindergarten, were assigned to the older building. Annie and Bonnie got to be in the newer building. Annie was a fourth grader and Bonnie was now in the fifth.

Bonnie liked to peer into the older building with its big double doors, reminding her of her first school days at the Cathedral School in Marquette. But this school was nicer because it was a public school. There was nothing Father could do about that; there was no parochial school on the north side of Copper Ridge.

Three days a week, all the Catholic children—and that was most of them on the north side—were dismissed an hour early so that they could attend catechism classes given by the nuns in another older, empty school building that had not yet been torn down. Its lower level was still usable though it was unheated. In winter everyone kept their heavy coats on, even the nuns wore long woolen capes over their habits and gloves with the fingers cut out, enabling them to write lessons on the cracked blackboards, the chalk often screeching on the worn surfaces.

This was catechism that Bonnie could take to heart. The commandments, the holy days, the precepts of the church, and holy pictures of the saints. Bonnie was finally entering into the mystery of faith. She treasured the holy pictures, with their tortured stories of martyrdom, and kept them in a fat scrap book. Kids were given those pictures as rewards for correct answers.

They sang, too, ancient chants; Gregorian, they were called, drawn with small square notes, tied together in groups of two and three on a four-lined staff. Another language. One cold afternoon, everyone had gone home except Bonnie, because she had been chosen to erase the black board and clean the erasers outside the door, a special privilege. She liked to hit the grey erasers together, watching the chalk dust fly, completing the task by lining the erasers in a neat row on the chalkboard ledge.

She decided to sit on the round stool in front of a pump organ, wanting to give it a try. She had watched the nun do it. It sounded by pushing firmly with her feet on the two wide pedals below the keyboard while her fingers pressed the keys up and down, steadily pumping, her feet never stopping or the mouth organ sound would quit. It was hard work. She fingered out one of the chants left on the music desk. "Mass of the Angels, Mode VIII," was the title. She thought she was alone, but a nun interrupted her, exclaiming, "Oh, you can read music!"

Her name was Sister Carol. She was everyone's favorite. She wore round-rimmed glasses, that made her eyes seem so pretty. Her face was cherubic, like the fairy godmother's in *Cinderella*, and her singing was sweet and birdlike. She seemed kindly, but Bonnie knew she could be stern, too, if the incorrect answer was given from the catechism. "Do you take piano lessons?" she asked.

"No Sister, I just figured it out by myself," Bonnie said, shyly.

This occasioned a visit to her father by Sister Carol—not at the bakery, but at the Italian Church of the Holy Martyrs, where Father was a faithful attendee. In fact, he had been asked to direct the choir, which he did, without pay, of course. Sister Carol told Bonnie's father that she wanted to give Bonnie piano lessons. She would charge one dollar a week, which Bonnie could earn by coming to their convent each morning before school and playing on their small electric keyboard while the nuns sang their chants during a private Mass in a small chapel in their convent next to the church. Father said this would work. Bonnie's first job. For pay! The electric organ wasn't pleasing to her ear, a toy really. She hated it.

To her surprise, she found that she would be receiving a dollar for each morning, five mornings a week, then every Saturday she headed for the rectory knocking on the door before confessions began and announced timidly to the parish priest that she was owed five dollars. The money was forthcoming, after an uncomfortable wait outside the door, and much grumping by the old priest as he handed the money over, all one dollar bills, hers to keep.

Bonnie used the money for lessons, sheet music, and Twinkies at the store kitty corner from the bakery. It was on the way to school. She stopped there each morning for this special treat. Antonio Crispignia, the store owner, was creepy. He had black, waxy, wavy hair, a squished looking flat face, and a sneaky way of making sure to put his hands on her arm or back as she paid her five cents. He was to be avoided. It was a cat and mouse game, in the door, getting the Twinkies, having the nickel ready, pulling away from the suggestive touch, and running out the door with her prize. She enjoyed every small bite, as she headed the next few blocks to the school.

That fifth-grade year was boring, except for the Christmas pageant, as Bonnie was chosen to be the Virgin. Jackie Fermo was Joseph. All the girls liked Jackie, so Bonnie was thrilled, even though not a word was spoken between them, but he held her hand, leading her as they wandered from the costume room to the manger set, where kids dressed as angels sang, and someone held a star over their heads. It was warm under the heavy make-up and costumes, and Bonnie felt a little queasy throughout the scene. Mama came to watch her that night, bringing Annie, Augie, and Allan.

Daddy couldn't come. He was the piano player in the Sammy Tomasi Band. Sammy and his wife Marla lived on Margaret street on the next block to the west. Marla was a wonderful cook and on more than one occasion sent the Smith's a dish of gnocchi, or ravioli, beginning Bonnie's life-long love of Italian food. Soon Mama learned to make Italian sauces, that was a break from the family's customary meal of mashed potatoes and salmon loaf with creamed peas and carrots. Bonnie liked her mother's usual meal too, though not as much as Italian spaghetti night.

The kerosene stove was gone now, replaced by an electric one with a special deep cooking burner for simmering sauces.

"I love your cooking, Mama," said Bonnie. "Especially the spaghetti."

"I'd better learn to cook Italian, Bonnie. We live in an Italian neighborhood. I like the food cooked that way, too. It's easier with the electric stove. And it's cheap. "Now get your things ready for school tomorrow. You'll need a sweater," she added brusquely. *She isn't much for praise*, Bonnie thought.

The Aridon school was a five block walk straight south from the bakery. It was usually an uneventful walk. Bonnie kicked the autumn leaves in little swirls, but mostly it was a cold walk through the winter months. Sometimes she'd get hit by an icy snowball thrown by the local boys. One time she was struck so hard on her cheek that she could hardly breathe with the pain, but she refused to let on that it hurt or even happened, only a few tears blurred her vision. Bonnie hated those boys and felt helpless. She vowed revenge. Stupid, mean boys.

Bonnie couldn't wait for sixth grade. She could hear the sixth graders singing *America the Beautiful* in three-part harmony, when she stood outside of their classroom door listening to their music class. Waves of wonder at the beauty of it washed over her.

Only Sister Carol knew of her musical inclination, and more importantly, she paired her with a girl in her grade who was taking voice lessons from Sister Carol. *Joanne. Joanne. Joanne. She is going to be my friend. My first friend in Copper Ridge.* She still thought of Charlotte and Ruthie, even Rita, but they were many miles away. She was hopeful about Joanne.

Bonnie played for her as Joanne sang, and Bonnie herself picked up some breathing skills during these lessons. *Breathe in, push down on the diaphragm, keeping the rib frame firm, don't let the breath out all at once.* Over and over Bonnie tried this exercise when she was alone, seeing how long she could hold a tone as she counted aloud, reaching as high as number twenty-five before taking another breath.

Bonnie thought Joanne sang a bit off key, like her own mother, but didn't comment on it. Painful as it was to listen as Joanne worked her way through *Songs My Mother Taught Me*, somehow Bonnie sensed that if she was to be useful as an accompanist, she had to keep her mouth shut. She also wanted to keep this new friend.

Joanne lived across the street a few doors north of the school. She was Italian and nearly pretty with straight, dark brown hair, eyes a little too wide set, and a mouth a little too close to her nose But the overall appearance was rather pleasing. She had a big brother, Tony, who was short and chunky, and a mother Bea, whose hair was dyed coal black, always in a braided bun, fastened high on the back of her head.

Her father's name was Georgio. He was a quiet man. Bonnie never heard him speak. After work, he sat every day at his kitchen table with the daily paper, carefully coloring in the b's, d's, e's, g's, o's, p's, and q's with a pencil until the whole front page was completed. Then he retired for the evening after finishing supper. He worked at the glider factory, too, like most of the men on the north side.

Joanne's brother, Tony, also worked at the same factory. Joanne said she had had another brother who was killed at the age of two when her mother poured a pan of scalding laundry water off the back porch, burning Paulo as he was playing unseen beneath the porch railing.

After that, the family enclosed the porch. There were metal venetian blinds in the porch windows. Bea washed each slat of the blinds every day. "There's so much dust," she complained. "I can't seem to get them clean." Sometimes Bea unhooked the blinds from the windows, not an easy task, and laid them out on the floor of the porch and kitchen, using a bleach solution to clean the cords which held the slats together. On those days, Joanne and Bonnie had to go in by the front door.

Tony wasn't home much, so Bonnie and Joanne loved to lie on

the floor of his small bedroom, reading his stacks of comic books, all forbidden to Bonnie by her father. "I disobeyed my father six times," became her weekly mantra in the confessional box.

Bea and her sister Pia walked several blocks to attend morning Mass—rain, shine, or mostly snow. Pia had one daughter, Joanne's cousin, Lucia, a blonde, stiffish looking, and stocky girl. Lucia's dad was the owner of Schneider's meat market. He was a butcher who could cut off the exact piece of roast portion a customer asked for— to the ounce.

He was fun to watch. Whack, whack, whack, tearing off the wrapping paper from a huge roll, wrapping the meat, taking a stubby pencil from behind his ear, and writing the price on the paper after putting the package onto the scale. Mr. Schneider had a round, thick body. He spoke little, but Bonnie sensed he was kind. Lucia was kind, too. She looked like her dad.

The Schneiders lived above the store, but Bonnie never got to go up there. The steps to their place ran alongside the store. She had to call up in a loud voice when she wanted Lucia to come down to join her and Joanne.

"Hey, Lucia, are you coming? We'll be late for school."

"Lucia, Lucia, c'mon down," Joanne would join in the chorus.

Finally, Lucia would appear with her mother, Pia, warning her to be careful on the steps. The steps were steep.

Pia and Bea went to the movies once a week on Sunday afternoon. They always took Joanne, Lucia and Bonnie with them. Pia paid Bonnie's way. Bonnie had to lie to Father when she was at the movies because most of them were not on the approved list of pictures on the "Legion of Decency," a list put out monthly by the Catholic Church. It was part of the *Catholic Register* newspaper to which Father subscribed. He liked to read what the Bishop had to say.

Condemned movies, movies showing divorce, infidelity or revealing gowns, were the worst. Bonnie put those titles on a mental list of forbidden things she longed to see. Bea did not take the girls to the condemned movies. Everything else was okay—Esther Williams, Van Johnson, June Allyson, Kathryn Greyson, Xavier Cugat, Carmen

Miranda, Bing Crosby and the Andrew Sisters. Life away from the bakery was broadening.

Around this time Sister Carol and Bonnie were moving forward with piano lessons on full throttle. Sister's big event was the student recital in the church hall above the catechism classrooms.

"I want you to play well, Bonnie," she cautioned. "You're my best piano student."

This expectation made Bonnie tense. She had trouble sleeping at night, thinking about how she would have to outshine everyone on the program, even Joanne.

Bonnie came to realize these recitals were more important to Sister than the catechism classes in the basement. For Bonnie these events were just as important. This would be her first public appearance as a pianist. The piano was an upright, some of the black keys were missing or sticky in the lower register, reminding her of the piano in Crystal Falls. That wouldn't affect her piece, except for one note in *The Poet and Peasant Overture,* thirteen pages long, memorized.

First on the program was Joanne, still singing off key, then the younger piano students, then Bonnie. Bonnie felt she was prepared to be Sister Carol's star. She knew the piece backwards and forwards. Nevertheless, for some reason her hands got sweaty as she sat there galumphing on the keys. Also, her left knee began to shake violently, causing her brain to forget all the notes. She kept pressing the keys down in a chromatic pattern until the music emerged in her mind's eye, and she continued the piece, skipping quickly to the end, reducing the thirteen pages to about nine. She was mortified. Her mother was there in her flat, yellow, pancake style hat. She held Bonnie's hand as they walked home, not saying anything. Bonnie was thankful that Daddy was playing a gig.

Chapter 21

The school dentist made his appearance. The county hired him to take care of children who could not afford to go to the dentist. That was most of the children on the north side of Copper Ridge. A school room was set up for his chair and other instruments of torture. The chair was black and had two pads attached where kids were supposed to place their heads as he stepped on a pedal which threw the back of the chair into a reclining position. Bonnie had never been to a dentist. Two by two, kids were led into the room to be examined and treated if the dentist discovered a cavity. Bonnie waited and watched as he probed Jackie Forno with his hooked metal, pointy stick, then produced a long needle and smiling at Bonnie said, "Watch, this doesn't hurt," He plunged the needle repeatedly into Jackie's pink gums.

Bonnie must have turned pale and she was told to come back later that afternoon. She walked out of the school, pleading a stomach ache that remained for the rest of the week, and she called Joanne each day to see if the dentist and his chair were gone, gone, gone.

"My tummy still hurts, Mama, I feel like throwing up all the time," she moaned convincingly every morning.

"You'll have to stay in bed then, Bonnie," said Mama. "Maybe it's a flu."

"Why is Bonnie not in school?" Daddy asked when he got home from work.

"It's some bug, Will." Mama said. The kids have had just about every catchy illness. I'm waiting this one out so there's no quarantine. There's no rash but she is running a little temp."

Bonnie had been making sure to drink a cup of hot water from the kettle on the stove before Mama came with the thermometer. That week she worked on her holy picture scrap book that contained her catechism rewards.

Most of the saint pictures were of martyrs who were stoned, shot with arrows, burned. Her favorite one was of St. Agnes, who had to ride a horse naked through the streets of Rome, her long beautiful blonde hair miraculously covering her private parts. St. Teresa, The Little Flower, was another favorite who had died young in a convent where her father had forced her to go, and she prayed all the time for sinners.

When she died, the story went, people prayed to her statue for healing and sometimes it worked. Her costumed statue was creamy white, flowing, topped with a black head dress that covered every part of her except her face and hands, hands that held a long black rosary. The statue stood on a pedestal in the Holy Martyr Church, though technically she wasn't a martyr. A bunch of fresh flowers was always at her feet, behind a stand of burning vigil candles.

Sister Carol let Joanne and Bonnie help in the church sacristy. "It's a great privilege to serve at God's altar," she told the girls.

They were often left to themselves. Their chore was to dig out the wax from every small vigil light glass that had burned down, then plop a new candle into the cleaned space. The vigil light stands held at least a hundred lights. There were ten statues of saints all around the side altars of the church with the vigil light stands in front of them.

A metal slot box was attached to each stand, where people dropped their coin in before lighting a candle, then made their prayer request on the kneeler before their favorite saint's altar. Ten cents. Bonnie had a lot of requests, but no dime. She rewarded her labors by relighting candles at each stand which had gone out before they had completely burned down.

"You shouldn't be doing that, Bonnie," cautioned Joanne. "Somebody might see you."

"The candle has to keep burning, Joanne, or the prayer doesn't stand a chance," retorted Bonnie. "It doesn't matter if there are more than one requests on the light." I'm doing the original dime a big favor."

"I guess so," said Joanne. "Here's one gone out. I'll light one, too." They both started to giggle.

Sister Carol did the large lamps, costing twenty-five cents. Those were lit if people were desperate about wanting prayers answered, as they burnt for at least five days. There was one extra-large lamp before the tabernacle containing the host. It hung high in the air, signifying the actual presence of the Blessed Sacrament. Only Sister kept that lit. She stood on a step stool, holding forth a long bronze stick with a burning wick flaming from the end. It was a special privilege. She was, after all, a bride of Christ.

The Copper Ridge nuns left in the summertime to return to their motherhouse. Bonnie didn't know what they did there. A lot of praying, she supposed. Sister Carol said that some of them would not be back. She wanted to go to the missions in Australia. Bonnie blew out a candle that was already lit then relit it, praying for Sister Carol's return to Copper Ridge.

"Saint Teresa, dear Little Flower," she prayed aloud, on her knees before the statue. "Please, don't send Sister Carol to the missions. Bring her back to Copper Ridge, please, please dear Little Flower." She added an Our Father and Hail Mary for good measure.

Summer passed slowly. Daddy still had his job. Mama didn't complain about not having enough money for food. Bonnie was overjoyed when Mama mentioned that Bonnie and Annie might go on a bus trip to Negaunee to spend another summer with Grandma Johnson.

"We can't let Bonnie go, Helen," said Daddy. "It's an extra expense, and I'm thinking about trading in the car for a newer model. Besides, you need her to go to the store for you."

That was the end of Mama's talk about what could have been another wonderful summer. Bonnie felt depressed by their decision. Everything became grey—Lake Wakesha, the movies with Joanne and Lucia, practicing the piano and the fruitless arguing with Augie and Alan. Augie had failed the third grade and had to do it over because his spelling was so bad. He and Alan, who had skipped two grades because he was so bright, were now together in third. Mother and Father talked quietly about this disgrace befalling the Smith family.

"Why didn't you help him, Helen? You signed his report cards. Did you think things would change after seeing the first one?"

"My hands are full all day trying to keep this place neat, Will. And why is it just my responsibility? You're part of this, too. When you're here you're always pounding away on the piano, stamping your foot so hard on the floor no one can get through to you. Bonnie has to pull on your sleeve and yell, 'Daddy, Daddy, when she wants help with her homework, and Augie doesn't even try to get your attention. At least Alan is doing well."

"Never marry a musician," she often told Bonnie. That didn't bother Bonnie, as she thought of herself as a musician, too. She was going to marry a rich man who liked music.

She had looked forward to the sixth grade, but except for the music class found it disappointing. Mrs. Anderson, the teacher was fearsome. Her eyes, enlarged by thick lenses always seemed to be looking at Bonnie. Bonnie liked to focus on the glass apple on the teacher's desk. It was beautiful, all reds and oranges. *I'd love to have that apple for myself,* Bonnie thought. *I'd look at it every day and then I'd feel happy.*

Bonnie wasn't happy about the gym classes either. All the running about and the sweating and most of all the communal showers.

"Marie Prianti is always excused from gym," she whispered to the all-knowing Joanne. "Why is that?"

"My mother said it's because she has the curse. It started when she was eight years old, humm" Joanne whispered back, between jumping jacks and squats.

"What's the curse, Joanne?" asked Bonnie.

"I'm not sure, Bonnie, but it's made her grow a little mustache over her lips."

Bonnie was growing a mustache, too, only it was 'down there'. Was she cursed, too, and might it get her out of gym class, she wondered? Who should she tell? The gym was full of girl mysteries.

Once Bonnie couldn't find one of her shoe's after showering. Trying not to look at the other naked girls, she searched worriedly for it, not realizing everyone else had left the shower room, until she heard the door close, followed by an ominous click.

She was locked in. Her heart pounded and she feared she would be there until the next day when another class came in. There was still a light on and, finally, she located her shoe under a few damp towels. She began to pound on the door, crying for help. After what seemed an eternity, the janitor heard her yelling and unlocked the door, shaking his head in sympathy. She ran to her classroom, late for music. Mrs. Brickly, the singing teacher, waved her to her seat without comment. Her classmates all had knowing smiles on their faces, even Joanne.

On the last day of the school year she returned to her empty school room and took the glass apple, putting it into her book bag along with all the useless papers which had been handed back to her, evidence of her scribbles over the past semesters, proof of her passing on.

When she got back to the bakery, she took Daddy's hammer from his tool drawer, put the apple on a cement block near the garbage can beneath the twenty-six steps and smashed it into a thousand pieces. She cut her little finger as she was scooping the pieces into the trash. *So much for pretty*, she thought, despondent.

Chapter 22

As the summer dragged on, Bonnie felt restless and uncertain about many things. She walked on warm days to Lake Wakesha, promising her mother not to hitchhike. She still had Aunt Lillian's swim suit, and now she filled it out a bit more, especially the top part. Joanne had one of the new two-piece suits, white with crisscrossing straps in the back. Bonnie was jealous of her smooth tan skin. She thought her own skin was too white, and it easily burned bright red in the sun, which did not stop her from applying baby oil that was supposed to produce a tan like the movie stars pictured in fan magazines.

Their pictures were also on the backs of ice cream Dixie Cups that all the girls collected. Lying there on the rocky beach, they talked of the girls who had to stuff Kleenex tissues into their suit cups to make them point forward. They didn't do much swimming.

"I've got Hedy Lamarr, Bonnie," bragged Joanne. "Will you trade me for Van Johnson, humm?"

"Maybe, Joanne," said Bonnie. I'll check my stack when I get home. I think I have two of Van Johnson. But if it's only one, I can't give *him* up."

Conversations were muted among the sun worshiping girls, the real conversations were never spoken but felt in the restless yearnings of their changing bodies

"I'm shaving my legs, now, humm" said Joanne.

Bonnie examined her legs, but saw only a light peachy fuzz. "I heard my mother talking to our neighbor. She said if you shave the hair will come back all black. I'll never do it," said Bonnie. She was fearful of cutting herself and seeing blood, but was mostly uncertain of how to go about it. There was only Daddy's razor. The shaving would take some careful planning. Bonnie knew she would shave the fuzz before seventh grade.

The lazy conversations continued with Joanne on the telephone every day, before and after school.

"Are you ready, Joanne? I'm leaving for school now. What are you wearing?"

"I'm wearing my new penny loafers today, Bonnie. How about you, humm?"

"I'm wearing my blue outfit. One of my aunts. She sent me two almost new things." Bonnie was proud of those dresses. They made her feel so grown up. *Seventh grade*, she thought. *I'll be a star in my grown-up clothes.*

All the grade schools in Copper Ridge went to the same Junior High building on the southeast side of town. Bonnie walked the distance—a long walk—stopping on the way for Joanne. The walk continued for several blocks, then crossed a bridge spanning deep, black water on either side, said to be the site of several drownings from which bodies were never recovered. Passing through the downtown area, they finally arrived at the school. The school building was new, built of pinkish smooth brick, three stories high, lined by classrooms on either side of long halls. *Who will be my enemy here?* Bonnie thought. *Will I find another friend?*

Sometimes on the mile-and-a half walk to school Joanne and Bonnie were joined by Janet, a neighbor who lived close by Joanne. Janet was a year ahead of them, a pleasant, plain, freckled girl, who added little to the conversation, that was mostly about boys and which teachers were supposed to be the best. By the best they meant the easiest. The downtown buildings had large posters with pictures of Uncle Sam pointing his finger saying I WANT YOU *or* BUY WAR BONDS. The signs unsettled Bonnie. *When will this war stop?* she wondered. *Why does there have to be a war?*

"My dad bought a twenty dollar bond," bragged Janet. "They're eighteen dollars I think, but he told my mom he would get the money back—with interest."

"I heard it's not for twenty years," said Joanne. "That's a long time to wait for twenty dollars. My mother said we're not buying any, humm."

Bonnie knew her daddy would not buy one, not with the new used car and the two-dollar raise in their rent payment. Her mother had asked her to contribute some of her organ playing money to help out. Her goal of being rich was beginning to seem like an impossible dream.

Adding to the tension of attending a new school and meeting new kids from the east and west side of town was the matter of the bra. Sister Carol did return. They were to continue with Bonnie's piano lessons. She commented one day on Bonnie's obvious breasts. They were starting to bounce if she ran or walked too fast.

"Tell your mother you need a brassiere!" Sister Carol quietly suggested one afternoon after the lesson was done.

"Oh, yes Sister, I will," Bonnie said but she didn't, feeling so embarrassed about her body, and hesitant to talk to her mother about such an intimate subject. Mama and Bonnie only talked about things that needed doing around the apartment.

Sister mentioned the problem to Daddy one Sunday, wondering why Bonnie was still not wearing a bra. Her world came crashing down when Daddy took her aside in the front room,

He berated and shamed her for not saying anything about needing a brassiere and lying about it. She was a liar, he said, and had compounded the lie by telling it to a *Sister. This sin was mortal*, she thought, *no doubt about that, and she would probably go to hell.*

She wasn't sorry about the lie, only about being shamed, which made her feel wretched for several days. She remembered the vigil candle she had lit for the return of Sister Carol. Now she regretted it. The prayer had back-fired in a terrible way. She wouldn't confess this.

Her eventual bra came from the five-and-dime store. She heard her daddy talking to Mama about the problem of the brassiere.

"Helen, didn't you notice Bonnie needed a brassiere?" said Daddy accusingly.

"Will, I've got a lot on my hands. Bonnie should have said something.

She needs to learn to speak up! She's a smart girl, she got an 'A' in every subject except gym last year," Mama jumped right back at Daddy, and then she began her usual crying whenever Daddy scolded her. "Brassieres cost money you know, she said through tears."

Daddy reached in his pocket and gave Mama three dollars. "Here," he said. "This should cover it."

Bonnie went alone to the dime store for the bra. The store had no dressing room so she had to guess a size. The clerk behind the women's underwear counter looked at her sympathetically.

"Here," she said, after Bonnie had stood there for several minutes, trying to look like she knew what she was doing. "This should be about right for you." She handed Bonnie the white garment wrapped in cellophane. "That will be two-fifty," she said. Bonnie kept the extra fifty cents, telling her mother that three dollars was the exact price of the bra.

Bonnie hated the bra. The thin straps cut into her shoulders, left red welts, but she did bypass the training bra size and wore one with real cups, which was greatly admired by still-flat, Janet.

"My mother says I'm a late bloomer," complained Janet. "You're so lucky. I'm jealous."

Bonnie was fascinated with her new figure. She liked to gaze in the bathroom mirror at her developing body. At the same time she was embarrassed by comments from her peers or her mother about her new look. She tried to conceal it by hunching forward when she walked.

"Stand up straight, Bonnie," Mama ordered. "Quit slouching. Stop dragging your feet. Here, put this book on your head and walk for ten minutes. You don't want to be a hunch back."

No, Bonnie thought, as she practiced with the wobbling book atop her springy Carla Romonogli curls. *I won't be a hunch back. I'm going to be beautiful and rich.* She was single minded about the rich part. Rich people were automatically beautiful and favored..

She compared herself to the pretty older girls on the town bus to school. She didn't get to ride the bus often. Sometimes the weather made it impossible to walk, for instance when it rained hard or when there was a blinding blizzard. Then Mama grudgingly came up with a nickel for the bus, which stopped a block east on Margaret Street at

8:05 AM and was not to be missed. Bonnie watched from the upstairs bakery window as the bus headed north on US 141, then she made a beeline down the twenty-six steps and ran to the corner bus stop across from Tramontine's store where the four ladies lived upstairs.

The bus stopped every four blocks on the north side of town. The prettiest girl on the bus was Patty Menucci. She was all smooth skinned, like warm butter, and her lips were pouty, perfectly drawn with a bright red color. The boys always tried to get a seat next to her. Bonnie was envious. Patty always wore her head scarf tucked just so, so that her dark hair would be perfect when it was removed. The scarf was so pretty. It was silky and printed with bright flowers. *If I had a scarf like that, boys would want to sit next to me, too,* Bonnie thought. *When I'm rich I'll have one even prettier.*

Other than the kiss on the skating rink in Marquette, she had never been among the chosen. Except for one thrilling time on the bus when handsome Teddy Dufresne, who had been standing, fell next to her by accident as the bus came to a sudden stop because of a big dog in the middle of the road. The driver had to leave his seat and pull the dog by its collar to the side of the road. He suffered a small nip to his hand, which wasn't a big deal, because he was wearing thick gloves due to the cold, though it got everyone on the bus laughing. Bonnie's hormones were in full gear, sitting next to Teddy. She ventured a "Hi Teddy." He paid her no attention at all.

Chapter 23

Blue capes and white veils, but not a May crowning. Annie and Bonnie were among the privileged to be members of the Holy Mary Sodality. They were supposed to look like the statue of the Virgin Mary. *An Army of Youth Flying the Banner of Truth* began the official song. A picture in one pile of papers in a shoebox, shows two rows of sixth, seventh, and eighth grade girls on the wide front steps of the Holy Martyr's Italian Church, on the north side of Copper Ridge. Sister Carol and Sister Gregory are on either side of the group.

Down the church aisle they paraded in pairs, the front two girls holding the blue and white *Sodality* banner on a high pole. Most of the girls had Carla Romongnoli permanents. Everyone was of an Italian heritage, with dark hair and light olive skin, except for the blonde Smith girls and Lucia Schneider. The three looked somehow out of place. The grocer, creepy Antonio Crispigna, tried to change the Smiths last name on the charge slips so their family would be more in keeping with the neighborhood. Smithini didn't work, nor did Smithorini.

Bonnie was the only one in the Sodality picture who wore glasses.

The parade was solemn as the song boomed out on the organ, and the little giggles and whispers didn't start until all were seated. They were all virgins, according to stern Sister Gregory, and were to remain so until marriage. Those entering the convent—and she hoped there would be more than one—would always be virgins. "You must always be on your guard," she cautioned at the monthly meetings which took place right in the church after the Mass. When she finished her speech, her face so serious throughout, there was always an embarrassed silence.

Bonnie wasn't certain how the virgin thing was to be maintained. Patsy Forno, Jackie's sister, an eighth grader, had to drop out of sodality because she was going to be married and have a baby. Her husband-to-be was a young man from Italy who spoke no English at all. *How did this translate into not being a virgin?* she wondered. *Does one have to have the baby first and then get married? Maybe Patsy was more like the Virgin Mary than any of us, but then why did she have to drop out?*

Joanne said Patsy wanted to get married, and she wanted to quit school, too. "She's already fourteen and she's failed more than one grade. She really should be in the ninth grade, humm"

Joanne is so smug, Bonnie thought. *Where does she get all her information?*

The Sodality girls went to communion first. Being a virgin was that important. Confession first, and then Communion. Bonnie wasn't sure if this would keep her out of hell, but there was another sure-fire way—the First Fridays!

No matter how many sins she had committed—and the priest said everyone, *everyone* was a sinner, except for that moment after baptism—if on the First Fridays of every month, she went to Mass and Holy Communion, being forgiven of her sins in confession, she would be certain of salvation, even skipping over Purgatory.

Bonnie was always starting over, uncertain of whether she maybe, had missed the previous month's Friday. This was a cause of much anxiety. Joanne said she had completed the task. Her mother had seen to it.

Bonnie's mother was oblivious to this ritual, even laughing in her beery chortle when Bonnie asked her one evening to help her to keep track of the First Friday dates.

"When would I have time for that? Sometimes, I don't even know what the date is myself. You play at the convent every morning. Surely you've made the First Fridays."

"What about summers, Mother? The nuns are gone then. I can never remember when I started."

"Check with you father, Bonnie Grace Smith. That's his sort of business."

Bonnie knew that when her mother said her whole name, that the conversation was at an end, but she persisted in trying to figure out her mother's seeming lack of faith.

"Don't you believe in God, Mama? Are you an atheist?" Bonnie had heard about atheists from Sister Carol. They were surely going to burn in hell forever.

"Of course, there's God, Bonnie Grace," said Mama, annoyed at being interrupted while setting out the dishes for supper. "What a silly question! Now help me put the leaf in the table."

Mama's always changing the subject when it comes to church, thought Bonnie She tried to picture herself in heaven, looking down at her mother screaming in the hot flames which didn't kill the lost souls, just tortured them forever. She knew she would be saved because of the special blessing given by the priest after Sodality meetings.

The priest came out from the sacristy and gave the girls this blessing, sprinkling holy water all over the group from his aspergillum. Bonnie loved that name. It reminded her of the asparagus she had had once at Aunt Tilly's. It tasted okay, but wasn't on her list of delicious foods, like the oysters her mother bought in the 'R' months around Christmas for the oyster stew. The aspergillum made water spots all over the flimsy blue capes. Annie loved her cape and managed to duck down so she could avoid the holy water.

"Stand up, Annie," Bonnie would whisper, appalled at the thought of Annie's not being saved.

But Annie wouldn't, despite Bonnie's insistent prodding.

"No, Bonnie. Quit poking me," pleaded Annie from her place under the pew bench. "I don't want those damn water spots all over me. We only get the one cape."

"Don't swear in church, Annie," whispered a horrified Bonnie. "Here comes the priest."

The priest always seemed to be annoyed about having to wait around after Mass. He would glare at Sister Carol and Sister Gregory while the sprinkling went on.

Chapter 24

Bonnie was afraid of a lot of things, but at the same time felt impelled to explore everything in her surroundings. She didn't want to go to hell; she wanted to go to Daddy's heaven. She wanted to have a good time and not have it be a sin. The Sisters seemed to be happy. Whenever she entered the convent through a side door for her lesson, she heard laughter from some closed off space. *Maybe I do belong in the convent*, she thought, *taking vows of poverty, chastity and obedience.* Could she be happy without being rich? What about poor people? Were they happy?

Three blocks west along Margaret Street across Highway 141, then across some railroad tracks, were a few small houses even shabbier than the ones heading east. The Bruno's, Caviani's, and Tomaso's, were the exception, being quite nice for the north side.

Those houses on the west side right next to the railroad tracks seemed to hold secrets. The kids playing outside were always smudged and raggedy looking. The mothers looking after the children seemed drawn and tired. Their shoulders sagged and their dresses hung open in a careless manner, as if they had been slept in, all wrinkly, buttons missing, hems hanging.

Bonnie realized her family had escaped this sort of area because of her daddy's job at the glider factory. She was reminded of the Piqua house and the bedbugs. Who were these families, she wondered? She never saw any of them in the grocery store. Where did they get their food? How did they get about? There was only one car in evidence, without tires, on wooden blocks. The kids let her play in the car with them. She pretended to drive, crying "toot-toot," every so often, because the horn didn't work. This made the little ones laugh, a tight sort of laugh. They all had dry coughs and snot running from their noses that dried on their faces.

The mothers nodded and called out a welcome when she came. "Hey, there, Bonnie. Nice to see you come by once in a while."

Bonnie wanted to run from this area, but felt captivated by this easy, relaxed atmosphere. No one seemed worried or out of place. They existed without seeming to have a care in the world. Mother said she should never go across the tracks. Joanne said the people in those houses were carnival people, gypsies. She said the town wanted them out. They did leave during the winter, and the houses would be empty. But they came back in late spring, sometimes with what appeared to be different children.

"My mother told me that they steal children, and they have catchy diseases, humm," Joanne said.

Bonnie didn't believe her. She thought they seemed odd, stilted, but there was a softness to them. The idea of a life that could disappear, then reappear at will was appealing to her, and never having to go to school was part of the appeal. School for the most part was such a trial. Always trying to figure out what her place was, jockeying for position, trying to be accepted as part of that milieu. Who were her friends? Who were her enemies? Maybe her runaway Uncle Pauly had the right idea.

Chapter 25

The part of school she did like was the library. It held so many answers, mostly in the *National Geographic*. Those magazines were well thumbed through and could be counted on to have at least two or three pages in the middle of the magazine of topless women and nearly naked men, except for a sort of chunky fabric around their man bulge, held on—God knows how—with a single strap in the crack of their bare buttocks.

There were glassed-in conference rooms in the library where no more than two students could ask to study together. Bonnie liked to go into one of these rooms with Barbara, (not the pale Barbara on Margaret Street,) but a cheery, round-faced Barbara who had so much forbidden knowledge to disperse in whispers, as they pretended to be looking at their textbooks while making funny doodles on their tablets.

"My sister got married last Saturday," Barbara said with a wide-eyed look that meant something amazing was about to be told. "There was a spot of blood on the sheet Sunday morning— in the bed— where she and her new husband had slept the night before." She whispered in a low, intimate tone, "That always happens on the wedding night. It hurts the woman"

Bonnie was dumbfounded by this new information and eager to learn more, but that's all Barbara knew. Bonnie was determined to learn more. The public library was another favorite place to search for the mysteries of the male and female anatomy. Pictures could be found in the medical section as well as in the *Encyclopedia Britannica*.

The library had the *Catholic Encyclopedia*, too, but there was no naked picture of St Agnes.

Mama sent Bonnie there every week to get the latest Faith Baldwin novels. They were Mama's favorite. The heroine's wardrobe was always described in detail and her and the misunderstood hero finally triumphed in a happy ending. Not like the dark fairy tales Bonnie liked to read after finishing her research in the anatomy section. A tale of toads instead of pearls tripping off lying tongues entranced her. Princes were sacrificed if they got the wrong answer, a beauty was forced to love a beast to save her family, sisters' feet were amputated to fit a shoe—there was always some terrible fate to befall the least favored. Only one character ever got the happy ever after. *That will be me*, she thought, *when I marry a rich prince.*

Her chance for romance arrived in the form of the seventh and eighth grade Friday night dances at the Ludington School, located on a hill on the east side of town in a poorly lit area. The dark shadows heightened the sense of adventure. That was a perfect place to explore as part of her quest for the yet unknown answers to her physical yearnings. Aunt Lillian's dance lessons came in handy as she moved and swung out with the other girls in jitterbug style. The space was rather small and dimly lit, causing the dancers to bump into one another while they laughed loudly, trying to attract the circle of boys who stood in nervous groups against the walls.

The boys rarely asked a girl to dance and then it was only during slow tunes. The juke-box music was loud and featured the popular tunes of the day. One boy—she couldn't remember his name—asked to walk her home one evening and she said okay.

He managed to hold her hand, his palm was hot, and as they passed by the Commercial Bank Building downtown, across from the train depot, he pressed her against the bank's rough stone surface, put his arms awkwardly around her and tried to kiss her. He was too short to manage anything graceful, but she did feel his bulge against her thigh as he tipped his mouth toward hers, only getting her chin with his closed lips. A volcano of warmth rushed over her whole body. She liked the sensation, but the moment didn't last long. *What was his name?* She tried to remember; it could have been Bud. During the encounter, she managed to slide his weekly bus pass from his jacket pocket. Stealing. A small sin for confession, she thought. Kisses would not be free

Bonnie felt desperate at times. She needed another source of money. The daily dollar earned at the convent was never enough to buy the penny loafers and angora sweaters which Joanne and Janet wore.

Mother said, "Bonnie you're now old enough now to get baby-sitting jobs on week-ends." She introduced her to her tavern friends, Homer and Ivy. They had a new baby and needed someone to watch the little boy on Saturday nights. They decided to hire Bonnie. They didn't live far from the bakery, so she could walk to their house, and Homer agreed drive to her home, which satisfied Daddy.

Homer was Hawaiian. Their baby had dark curly hair and might have been cute except that he cried a lot—screamed really—refusing to take the offered bottle of carefully warmed milk. Bonnie finally just let him cry himself to sleep in his crib, and being tired herself, as it was getting late, she decided to lie down on the tan plastic-covered couch with one yarn, ropy, lime-hued cushion propped on each end. It was in the room just off the kitchen, not far from the nursery door.

Just as she was dozing off, she felt hot breath on her cheek and heard a sputtering voice murmuring incoherently, as a hand moved over her breast. It was the old grandfather. She hadn't been aware that he was in the house. In a panic she pushed him aside, saying the baby was crying, though he wasn't, and she ran into the nursery, slammed the door shut, and put a small chair under the door knob. She didn't know where the old man went. He didn't try to come in. She stayed there, sitting tensely by the crib of the sleeping child until Homer and Ivy came home. Ivy had left a silver compact on the baby's dresser, so Bonnie pocketed it in payment for having to stay locked in the nursery. She had no need for the compact and didn't even want it, but the rebellious act assuaged her anger at life's unfairness, at least for a little while.

"How did everything go?' Homer asked on the drive home.

"Fine," she said, as he gave her two dollars.

She didn't say anything to Mother about her experience, but she never went there again, and she disposed of the compact under a bus seat, on which she rode using the weekly pass she'd filched from Bud, which she thought was his name. Yes, that was his name. Bud.

Chapter 26

Except for the sodality picture, there are no photos of Bonnie in junior high, not even a school picture. There are no pictures of anyone in her family either.

Where were Augie and Alan? Bonnie was so wrapped up in herself that she only noticed them when she was called on to baby sit. Augie liked to work on ten-cent, balsa wood airplane kits. There were so many little pieces, punched out from flat square sheets, like paper dolls. He had failed another grade, and now Alan was ahead of him.

Alan was the brains in the Smith family. Quiet and rather short, but all the boys seemed short to Bonnie. His hair was enviably curly and his head was always in a book. His nose had a little tic that moved back and forth twisting his mouth to the left. He was quick to cry if reprimanded. He spent a lot of time at the church learning the Latin prayers for altar boys. Father said he would be a priest one day. He was Mother's favorite.

Augie seemed happy enough, always singing *Mexicali Rose* at the top of his voice as he rounded the corner, coming back from wherever. He ate scads of mashed potatoes and was a growing boy despite his childhood illness. He was almost as tall as Bonnie, and he liked to give her a punch or two whenever she was the sitter while Mama was at her new entertainment of choice—bingo—and Daddy was playing a gig.

The Ford glider plant paid well, and Daddy bought Mama a curly black lamb fur coat which she wore with a two-piece black dress, the blouse's edge scalloped with white scrolled trim. Bonnie doesn't need a picture to remember how beautiful Mama looked in that attire, all dressed up to go out to the bars with Daddy.

Once Mama went out with Della and Daddy was the only one home. Bonnie was practicing *Malaguena* a piece that fully expressed her romantic longings, when, suddenly, she felt a strange warmth flooding her undies. She raced to the bathroom, bypassing Daddy who was at the kitchen table absorbed in writing music arrangements for Sammy's band. The rush of blood coloring the toilet bowl scared the wits out of her. *Is this the red spot? I'm not married,* she thought, *and this is a lot more than a spot*! She heard the screen door—Mama at last.

"Mama, come in here," she pleaded in a loud whisper from the slightly opened bathroom door, where she could see mother as she entered. Mama put her handbag down on the kitchen table and came into the bathroom. Bonnie was embarrassed, as it had been years since Mama had been in that room with her. She may never have been, as far as Bonnie could recall.

Mama went to one of the bureau drawers and fished out a belt with hanging straps, front and back, ending with metal clips, which she put around Bonnie's waist. "It's ok." she said. "You put this pad between your legs." She took it from a box, just like the one Bonnie had been sent to buy in Crystal Falls. "This will happen for four or five days every month until the bleeding stops."

Now Bonnie knew what these pads were for. Dark bleeding. *Not good. Misery. Yuck,* she thought. She didn't yet know why this had to happen. She was not happy and her stomach hurt.

She called Joanne later that night and told her what had happened.

"It happened to me, too, Bonnie, just a few days ago, humm." said Joanne, importantly. "My mother said it's the curse. If I'm not careful I'll have a baby, humm."

"Are we still virgins, Joanne? I'm afraid to ask my mother," said Bonnie.

"That's all my mother told me," said Joanne. "I'll ask Janet. She's older and probably knows the whole story. Talk to you tomorrow."

Chapter 27

Returning to the eighth grade after that summer was exciting and mysterious. Boys who had been shorter than Bonnie now had long, gangly, uncertain legs, which created a funny picture to her eyes, especially when they were coming down the stairs in a knee bent robotic walk. Even their faces seemed different.

"Did you recognize Jackie Forno, Joanne?" she asked on the before school morning phone call. "He's got funny fuzz all over his face."

"And pimples, too," Joanne answered. "He's still kind of cute, though. I noticed you had a blackhead on your nose. Better squeeze it out, humm"

Bonnie had been painfully squeezing out the intruders on her skin. Joanne didn't have any on her smooth olive completion and that made Bonnie jealous.

"My dad said to put soap on my face and leave it dry until it's a stiff mask," Bonnie bragged to Joanne. Then I must leave it on for ten minutes before washing it off with warm water. It's better than squeezing, he said." Bonnie knew Joanne's dad never said a helpful word. *My dad is better than Joanne's dad,* she thought, *and handsomer, too.*

"I'm leaving for school now. Be by in five minutes," Bonnie said. "I'm taking my new school bag. It's green"

"Mine's green, too," Joanne said. I'll be outside waiting for you. Don't be late, humm"

"Remember our lessons with Sister Carol, today," said Bonnie on Mondays. She always had to remind Joanne.

Sister Carol continued Bonnie's piano lessons and pushed the idea that she should enter the convent after eighth as a postulant in their school for girls in Chicago.

"The school only accepts devout girls like you, Bonnie." Then she warned in her sweet voice, "You'll never be happy as a married woman,"

Bonnie was eager to go. She hated school and wanted an adventure after the long boring summer.

"I'm going to enter the convent," she told Joanne.

"I want to go, too," said Joanne.

Why does Joanne always want to do the same thing as me, thought Bonnie? *This is supposed to be my adventure.*

"Well, of course, Joanne, you've probably already talked to Sister Carol about becoming a nun," Bonnie said. She was quietly furious that Sister Carol had said something to Joanne. *Had Sister talked to Joanne, first,* she wondered?

"We'll have to ask our parents for permission, Joanne," she warned, knowing Joanne's mother would never let her leave Copper Ridge."

Bonnie pleaded with her father, "Please, please, Daddy, I want to be a nun."

But Daddy said," No, Bonnie. I'm sorry, you're needed at home to help your mother with your younger brothers."

It didn't seem to Bonnie that her brothers were in any need of help. Augie had his airplane kits and Alan was always into a book. *Why couldn't Annie be the helper*, she thought? *Annie gets away with everything.*

Annie was the belle of the ball with her new set of bold girlfriends. Bonnie hated and feared Daddy now because of the bra incident and because of his refusal to let her go to the convent. She and Joanne would just have to get through the eighth grade and go to the town's high school like everyone else. Nothing exciting or special.

At least Bonnie had one favorite class in Middle School—chorus. The teacher recognized her music reading abilities and asked Bonnie to be part of the select girl's trio, singing the alto part with another girl, Paula, who sang the middle voice, and of course Joanne singing the soprano, still slightly off key despite her voice lessons from Sister Carol. At last, some special attention.

The trio was called the *Three Little Maids*, which was their theme song. Paula was a sometime joiner on the walk to school, a lusty girl who had overnight pajama parties in her attic over the gas station apartment where she lived with her younger sister, Bernadette, and her mother and father. Paula's father owned the station. Bonnie was thrilled to be invited to one of Paula's parties, but shocked when Paula would stoop and pull down her pajama pants to show the other girls her bare bottom. She called it "mooning."

"I've sneaked into the boys' locker room and done it, too," Paula boasted.

Should Paula confess this or should I, Bonnie wondered? *Surely this was not right.* She didn't think Paula cared a whit about sinning. Paula was part of the popular crowd. Her father owned a moneymaking property which seemed to exempt her from all wrong. That's what having money did for a person. Bonnie would have money someday too, when she left the bakery. She had given up on the idea of becoming a nun and so had Joanne. Being rich was more important.

Bonnie's was still looking for ways to get more pocket money. She envied Joanne's liberal allowance. There were still two years before Bonnie would turn sixteen, the legal age for working in the dime store—her dream job as there were so many pretty things on display—so she decided to try the bakery owner, Tolly, for any kind of job.

Her parents rarely saw him, except when he came to collect the rent. Bonnie and Annie had often ventured inside the bakery and were sometimes given a free, crooked donut dipped in powdered sugar, The sugar came from huge cardboard barrels held together by shiny metal bands at the bottom and top. The bakery guys, in their white aprons and caps, liked to tease Bonnie in a friendly way. Bonnie liked their silly banter.

"Here she is, the princess living above us," one of the guys might say, or, "C'mon over here, we'll let you punch the bread dough down."

One time she did. Rising in troughs, the smooth, white, living, dough reminded her of the dough in her grandmother Johnson's mixing bowl. Bonnie had watched her punch it down, turn it, and knead it, even helping a little.

Bonnie was enthusiastic as she started to flail away at the task, although soon became overwhelmed by the carbon dioxide fumes and other yeasty things. The guys all hooted as she staggered out the door. She was sick for several days from the smell; but she went back below. Tolly, the boss, knowing what had happened, seemed apologetic.

"Hey, Bonnie," he said, "Come on to the packaging room, we need some help there. I can give you and Annie fifty cents a day, cash, for coming here after school for just an hour to frost and wrap the danish rolls in half-dozen packages."

The frosting was in the same sort of large barrels as the powdered sugar. The danish rolls were on metal racks on heavy baking sheets, each sheet holding four dozen rolls. The cellophane wrapping was on a gigantic roll. Annie, after much persuasion, took the job with Bonnie for the next school year. It was kind of a fun activity, slapping the frosting with their bare hands onto the sheets of rolls, splitting them into groups of six, tearing the cellophane off, putting the buns just so on the wrapping, folding, then placing the packages on a hot plate, to seal them, finally stacking them onto another rack, to be rolled out to the delivery van.

Tolly turned out to be not so nice. Whenever it suited him, he occasionally came by to check their progress and managed to deliver little pinches to Bonnie's backside.

So, this is what I'm really being paid for, she thought, but the extra money added to the five dollars for the morning organ stint at the convent meant she could buy a new sweater or skirt. Aunt Lillian had continued to send her castoffs, but she so wanted to have her very own, never- worn clothes.

Annie was always hungry. Her favorite thing on the job was to lick the frosting from her fingers every so often. She couldn't eat the buns because Tolly knew just how many there were, and she didn't want to make him mad. He had an awful temper, and all the guys who worked for him would jump to it when he was around.

When he wasn't around, there were knowing looks, comments, and guffaws about his whereabouts. They knew about Angeline, his girlfriend, who he bought things for and took for rides in the bakery van along the delivery route. Angeline was a bartender at the Riverside Club.

She wore low cut blouses with no bra, showing everything including her nipples when she bent over to get a bottle from below the bar. Tolly was there most nights.

His wife, Celia, knew about his wanderings, people said, but she just stayed home most of the time, taking care of their five kids—two of them twins—and kept the house in good order in case the parish priest stopped by, that happened more often that it should have, according to local gossip.

Bonnie was still not where she wanted to be—mainly not rich—and she recognized that the path ahead, through the many streets of Copper Ridge, would require a lot more, maybe dangerous explorations.

On Margaret Street, time had shifted things a bit. Mr. Columbo and his daughter, Barbara had moved from their rundown house after Mrs. Columbo died in a particularly severe asthma attack, as Barbara had predicted. Bonnie didn't know where they had gone.

The city condemned the house and it was torn down, leaving an empty lot with nothing but prickly weeds. Mr. Marconi had finally turned completely to stone and died. Carla Romonogli still had her front porch beauty shop with the clothes on hangers displayed in the window, but Mr. Romonogli never did return from the oil fields.

The mysterious ladies were no longer above the Tramontine store at the end of the block. People said they had moved to a green-shingled house out on Highway 141. It was called the Green Door, not far from the Riverside Club, where Daddy played a lot of jobs on weekends.

Crispigna's store had added a wooden shed-like structure to the back of the store, where people could buy jugs of home-made wine or grappa. Sometimes they just sat around at the few small tables and played cards for money.

That was the meeting place for The Sons of Venice. The members had to be first or second generation Italian men to belong to this organization. They celebrated certain saint's feast days, usually St. Anthony's, by hiring Mrs. Prianti, the best Northside cook. She made them their polenta and sausage. Mrs. Prianti had her coterie of women helpers, among them Tolly's wife, who helped with all the cooking and serving. As women couldn't partake in the festivities, they hurried out when glasses were raised and the singing of *O, Sole Mio* began.

The women would come back the next morning to clean up before the store officially opened.

Copper Ridge High School 1946-1952

Chapter 28

Bonnie was hoping for a change in social status when she walked into the high school building. There is one picture—just one—of the ninth-grade class. There were one hundred and twenty kids in Bonnie's class. She is shown standing in the back row—being one of the taller ones—wearing a loose blouse with short puffy sleeves, one of Aunt Lillian's. Her hair is bushed out with one of Carla's perms. Joanne, being of average height, though still on the chubby side was in the front row.

"My mother's going to buy a copy of this picture," Joanne said. "They cost two dollars for the big one. She wants it for her photograph album. She has pictures of me from every birthday since I was a new baby, humm"

Bonnie had seen the album. There was one picture of Joanne posed on a fluffy blanket, stark naked. Bonnie was glad there were none of herself at that age. She thought of the picture taken with Grandpa Johnson, her snug bonnet on, concealing her protruding ear.

"My mother says she has enough pictures of me," Bonnie said. "I'd rather have the two dollars for a new lipstick and matching nail polish. Red. Did you see the new permanent wave kits?" I think Carla's going to go for those now." They only cost two dollars, too. Bonnie knew there was no photographic record of her life and was glad of it. She would start her album when she reached her goal of becoming rich.

Bonnie still met Joanne for the long walk to school, listening to her talk about the new dress being made for her based on a picture in *Seventeen Magazine*. Bonnie quickly discovered that the cliques had already been formed, and again, she wasn't where she wanted to be.

Joanne, because of her beautiful, popular older twin cousins, who did fantastic cheerleading stints at all the games, swishing their pompoms, jumping up and down in their short black-and-gold pleated skirts, could move back and forth between the poor north side kids and the privileged east and west-siders. Bonnie's classmates had never heard of her elementary school.

Bonnie's ability to play the piano was her redeeming quality. The choir director, Mr. Beaverson, who also led the band and orchestra, knew Daddy, because they sometimes played gigs together in the Sammy Tomasi orchestra. Mr. Beaverson played the clarinet. Daddy bragged about Bonnie's playing skills, so Mr. Beaverson asked her to be the accompanist for orchestra classes, bands and choirs groups. Mr. Beaverson was a handsome, tall, blond, red-faced Swede and Bonnie had a huge crush on him. All the girls did.

I'm his star in chorus, humm" said Joanne.

"What about our girls' trio, Joanne?" reminded Bonnie. He's always asking the three of us to sing for assemblies. No. Shelly's his favorite. He drives her to school, and she has really big breasts."

"Is that all you can talk about, Bonnie? Big breasts, humm?"

"You're just jealous, Joanne, because I have him for three classes. I'm heading for orchestra right now. See you after school, Ok?"

They parted in somewhat of a huff.

Even with the acknowledgement of her piano playing abilities, she recognized that she was doomed to be an outsider, forever looking on at the put together girls who took charge of everything. They didn't live over a bakery, but in white houses with wide wrap-around porches, up and down hilly streets that were broad and fronted with un-cracked sidewalks. Oddly, no one ever sat on these porches, though there were porch swings in evidence.

Bonnie was a bright student, bringing home report cards with many 'A's' and sometimes a 'B'. The 'B's' were in geometry and chemistry. Her chemistry lab drawer was filled with broken pieces of pipettes and test tubes that she tried to hide. They were the result of failed experiments. Once, trying to make cold cream, she had used boric acid instead of borax, resulting in a beaker of wax, which she dumped it into the grey, iron lab sink. The wax clogged the drain and caused Mrs. Dunmar, a usually unflappable woman, to lose her temper.

"Look what you've done, Bonnie Smith," her face grew all red as she poked at the waxy mess in the sink practically screaming at her so everyone could hear. "The directions say borax, not boric acid

"I'm sorry, Mrs. Dunmar," stammered Bonnie, embarrassed. She felt her face redden, too.

"Well, you'll have to be late for your next class. This must be cleaned at once," Mrs. Dunmar ordered as she took out her detention pad and filled it out with Bonnie's name. "Take this to the office when you've finished."

Bonnie's next class was orchestra so Mr. Beaverson would have to teach the strings without having the piano to give the violins the illusion that they were playing in tune. Bonnie loved orchestra. It got her out of gym class and was the bright light of her freshman year. She hoped she wouldn't run into Mrs. Dunmar again when she entered the tenth grade.

Mrs. Dunmar was the mother of one son, Bob, who took Joanne to the prom during sophomore year. Bonnie went, too, with Bobby Romongnoli, the same boy who had exposed himself to her from behind the bakery only a few years before. Bonnie couldn't believe he had asked her, but he was the first one to invite her and he had grown out of his early fatness. *I'll try to put that out of my mind, she thought. Maybe he's forgotten it, too.*

She wore a borrowed dress, pink and pretty. Joanne's mother had gotten it for her from Lucia, so it was a little big on her. Bonnie and Bobby doubled with Joanne and Bob. Mr. Dunmar was the driver. When they arrived at the dance, the boys filled out the girls' dance cards that the girls then hung from a golden cord around their wrists. Bonnie hoped Bobby would ask some of the cute guys to dance with her as she watched him get her card filled out before the music started. There were ten dances in all.

Bonnie's card started with Mr. Egessi, the social studies teacher, whom no one wanted to dance with because he had a bad reputation. She had heard it from Joanne.

"He's known for holding the girls too tightly and moving his big hand up and down their backs. My mother said he's a strange guy, humm"

That's a mean thing for Bobby to do, thought Bonnie, when she looked in dismay at her dance card. Bobby only had his name down for the last dance and she was glad when the prom was over. She felt miserable.

After the dance, they went to Mrs. Dunmar's house for an after party. Bonnie felt out of her depth socially, but she carefully observed her surroundings, noting that the Dunmar house was a lot nicer than Joanne's, or Grandma Johnson's. *They must be rich*, thought Bonnie. *I want to be rich, too.* I'm so tired of wearing hand-me-downs, having to wear the same skirt day after day, while pretending to be dressed in fashion. She thought everyone in her class looked at her as unworthy.

I'm in the wrong group, she thought. She wondered what the key was to get into the popular clique, besides being rich. Her sister Annie was already doing fine with the fun, fast group, who stood outside at dances, grabbing a smoke, flirting with boys, skipping school, at times getting expelled, generally rebelling and having a good time.

Annie's friends' world was appealing, but scary. Sometimes Mama would say, "Annie, take Bonnie with you."

Annie would groan and say, "Do I have to?" But on these occasions Bonnie didn't fit in with Annie's crowd, either.

Chapter 29

Bonnie and Annie grew apart. At the times when they worked in the bakery—dodging Tolly and deliberately burning the bottom wrappers of the danish rolls whenever Tolly succeeded with a pinch—they sometimes regained their childhood closeness.

Augie, who now liked to be called Gus, was in another world, having been taken under the wing of his English teacher. Mr. Gorman insisted that, yes, Augie was a bright kid, and he helped him maneuver through the tenses, pluperfects, past perfects, and perfects, common nouns, proper nouns, and all of that. He even took Augie to the airport on many occasions, knowing of Gus's hobby of making airplanes from the balsa kits. Mr. Gorman, in addition to being an English teacher, was also a pilot. He owned the Gorman warehouse, which rented freezer lockers to local hunters who were fortunate enough to get their yearly deer kill. They needed a place to store the resultant steaks, chops, and roasts in the freezer lockers.

Gus looked so handsome in his class pictures, with his dark blond, wavy hair and dimpled chin. He and Alan could have been twins, except that Alan was a head shorter and even blonder. Even though Gus's clothes weren't the newest, he seemed to be happily self-contained. All the girls liked him.

Mr. Gorman saw to it that Gus also had the necessary ski equipment for the local, small mountain, where everyone went after school during the long snowy season. Bonnie did, too, in whatever borrowed equipment she could finagle. Grabbing onto the rope tow was challenging. Her arms always ached as she clung tightly, bumping over the dips to the top of the hill.

She never skiied straight down, being fearful of breaking something. Her long wooden skis were so clunky, and the borrowed boots didn't quite fit. She envied Gus's sleek new skies and smart jacket. Bonnie saw that Gus had moved up in the world, thanks to Mr. Gorman. She was glad for him, but she wished someone would give her new ski clothes, too.

Allen skipped yet another grade. Mother coddled him, always bragging about how smart and handsome he was with his girlish good looks. Alan took Mother's favoritism in stride, using his position to get away with little nonsense tricks and teasing. He was a reader, like Bonnie, but he preferred political stuff and science fiction. He and Bonnie argued at times. "Science fiction is just fairy tales," she would insist.

"Hey, Bonnie, you've been living in a fairy tale your whole life, waiting for a fairy godmother to transform you into a rich beautiful princess. When will you wake up? And all the religious crap, that's a fairy tale, too. *Hocus Pocus, Dominocus,*" he would tease her. Bonnie had no answer for his God taunts. Church was important for her, but she couldn't seem to come up with the perfect response to combat Alan's growing disbelief.

Hocus Pocus. Dominocus was Alan's cry when he worked one of his magic tricks—with cards mostly, but sometimes with magic boxes and steely ring puzzles. That was his hobby. Even though he was only twelve, he seemed older because he had skipped so many grades. He had a part-time job at a local gas station washing windshields and checking oil. He spent his small earnings on magic tricks from the local game store. Also on caps. He loved to wear different color caps. When listening to Detroit Tigers games on the radio—that was his favorite team—he wore the cap which had their team name prominently displayed on the front.

Father loved the Tigers too. That was the one thing he and Alan agreed on. Father had become more obsessive about his Catholic faith, still going to confess his sins every Saturday. He held himself strictly to the precepts of the church, like Easter Duty, and no meat on Friday, that were on the list of the six church laws. Mama observed the no meat Friday, but still was not a church-goer. Father had stopped pressing her to attend Mass. He prayed for other sinners during the nightly dreaded family rosaries. He kept the radio on during these pray times if the Tigers were playing. The radio ball games were good for putting Bonnie to sleep.

Father said his older brother, Uncle Francis, had been an announcer for the fights at one time, as well as other sporting events in the Detroit area, until one morning he was found dead. He was only forty-two years old. Father said he drank too much.

Bonnie couldn't remember ever seeing Uncle Francis, but thought that was why Father was so fond of the Tigers, Uncle Francis having died in Detroit and all of that. Aunt Lillian said that's where the Smith family had adopted Grandpa Ollie.

Bonnie no longer went to catechism. Instead, she went to Catholic Youth Organization meetings and dances in the same northside catechism building, on the upper floor, where she had failed so miserably at the piano recital. CYO was about Catholic boys and girls getting together for dances, chaperoned by the young assistant parish priest. The young priests were always good looking, and they liked to dance, too. People said they got moved around so often because the old pastor was so hard to get along with.

Bonnie could understand this, as she had to confront him when asking for her organ-playing money. He wasn't nice to the nuns either. *Why is there a barrier between these holy people who dedicated their lives to God,* Bonnie wondered? Annie didn't attend these dances, nor did Alan or Gus.

Oh, those religious rules. Father was impossible to argue with at times. Bonnie listened, fasinated, when he and Mother went back and forth about whether cream of mushroom soup could be used in the Friday tuna casserole.

"Will, there's no meat in this can," she insisted.

"Yes, there is, Helen. Look on the label. It says right here, extracts. I don't know what that is." Still, Mama served the casserole and he ate it, then fumed around until the next day's Saturday confession. He was always in that dark box a long time.

Maybe he does sin a lot, Bonnie thought, *out playing in the bars every weekend*. She would waken when she heard him coming up the twenty-six steps at 2:00 AM, then watch him from the bedroom door as he knelt for the longest time, head bowed, his arms resting on the corner of the kitchen table.

By that time, Alan was refusing to go to Mass. He and Father had terrible arguments about this. They were loud. Mama would lock herself in the bathroom during these shouting matches. There was no giving on either side. Alan was too big now for Father to whip him with his strop, and Mother was glad of that fact. She still didn't attend church or take part in the after supper family rosary.

Mama was rounding out in a sort of vanilla pudding-like way. She seldom went with Will to his gigs, instead going with Della, her neighbor, to the church bingo games four nights a week. They took the bus together to the Catholic Church on the south side, St. Joseph's. As she got rounder, Bonnie thought her less beautiful.

In the afternoons, she napped on the couch with a newspaper over her face. Evenings, when there was no bingo, were spent drinking her quart of Bosch beer and playing cards with the neighbors. There were loud arguments at times, as Daddy had to replay every hand, pointing out who should have played what, especially when he and his partner lost.

"Let it go, Will," Mama would admonish. "We're here for a good time. Just deal the cards." But Daddy wouldn't let it go, and Mama would give a sigh of defeat. She and her partner, Della, would light up their cigarettes until the hand was finally settled.

Della had a restaurant downtown, and she persuaded Mama to come and work for her on the weekends. It was an Italian place. The family meals became so much better as Mama learned to cook this new cuisine. Meat and potatoes were often replaced with spaghetti and meat sauce. They still ate the tuna casserole mixed with the questionable soup on Fridays.

Chapter 30

Bonnie's newest friend, Alice, played the violin in the school orchestra. Alice rarely played in tune and she wasn't one of the popular girls. She was rather homely, but her mother encouraged friendships by hosting weekly Saturday afternoon gatherings at Alice's house.

Bonnie and Alice always played a board game or Crazy Eights, followed by snacks of various assortments of cookies and cocoa. Sally and Shirley, two East-siders in Bonnie's class along with Joanne now formed a gang. They called themselves The Green Dots. They drew little green dots on their hands and school notebooks.

Alice's house had comfortable chairs, couches, nice end tables and pretty lamps. Bonnie could envision herself there, although she still wanted more.

The Green Dots were now recognized by their peers as an exclusive group. They had become even a little desirable to some of the real outsiders. One girl Betty Sparda, was always trying to be part of their little club. She lived on the northside, too, like Bonnie and Joanne, so on occasion they would let her walk home with them. Once, as they were approaching her house, a shabby structure with no basement, and bare cement floors throughout, Betty's mother called them to come in.

She offered them a tray of cookies and Jell-o cubes. The house was chilly inside. Furniture was sparse and the floor was icy, giving up threads of cold, making the few metal chairs uncomfortable to sit on. Bonnie kept her mittens on and her scarf tight around her throat. She took one of the cookies, but passed on the wobbly cubes.

Betty was a frail, pimply-covered girl, with stringy hair, and she always had a slouchy way of walking, perhaps to accommodate her baggy clothing, certainly not as nice as those Bonnie got from her from Aunt Lillian. After leaving Betty, Bonnie and Joanne weren't kind in their snide, superior remarks about her during their usual afterschool phone calls.

"She'll never be a Green Dot," pronounced Joanne. "She's too strange, humm"

"Your so right, Joanne," said Bonnie. "Strange is a good word for her. It's not her fault, though. Her mother is the same way. They both have a funny lisp"

"Yes, that lisp, good one, Bonnie. Did you notice how her tongue sort of sticks out when she talks, humm?"

"I did," said Bonnie. Bonnie felt guilty after hanging up the phone. Why did she always go along with Joanne's assessments of someone's flaws? *Does Joanne talk of me to others in this disparaging way*, she thought? *Is my going along with her and even adding to her mean words a sin?* What commandment would that be? *Maybe it goes along with Thou Shalt Not Kill. I'll ask the priest in confession. Or maybe Sister Carol.*

Sister Carol was interested in The Green Dots. She wanted to know what they did together. Bonnie said they were a knitting club.

"We knit scarves for the Catholic relief effort," she lied off the top of her head.

"That's wonderful, Bonnie. A noble enterprise," Sister said.

Not one of the Green Dots could knit. They spent their time together, talking about boys— who was hooked up with which girl, and pretending shock at the break-ups. On bus rides to out- of-town games, they were loud and giggly, acting so wise and important. Bonnie felt a sense of belonging when she was with them, but she found herself pretending she was as well off as her friends, and knew she was being false. Not her real self. She envied their evidently easy way of planning to buy a new skirt or sweater. *Are they pretending, too*, she thought?

Bonnie's improved dancing skills, were still not as good as Annie's. They both danced on Friday nights at Al's Juke Box Joint located on the far the south side. These days Bonnie had no lack of partners. Al's was dimly lit and the small floor meant the crowd was pressed together like the earlier dances at the Ludington school. The owner threw corn meal down regularly to make dancing easier. No liquor was served but one could by a Coke or Pepsi from the soda machine in the corner. Boys went in and out and laughed importantly as they returned with beery breaths.

One boy, Eddie, was often drunk and he had to be propped against a wall, so he didn't fall over. Some girls seemed to like Eddie. "Hey, Eddie," they would say in an admiring way, "can I get you anything?"

"Want me to come home with you?"

"Like your haircut, Eddie." Things like that.

Eddie even kept beer in the high school basement book-locker room. Bonnie watched with envy at the going steady couples making out between classes with sweaty fumblings and pressings. She wanted to be part of this scene, but at the same time was afraid. Sister Carol was still telling her stories about the wonders of convent life.

"Yes, Sister, I'd like to join the convent, but Mother says I'm needed at home." That was another lie she told, a small one for confession. Bonnie didn't want to be a nun, but Sister Carol wouldn't find out because she didn't talk to Daddy anymore. Daddy spent his after church time talking to the parish priest..

Everyone in the family was busy. Gus was with Mr. Gorman at the airport, Mama was at the restaurant or bingo, Daddy was out playing gigs, Annie was with her fast crowd, and Alan was with his books. They were all exploring in their own way. Bonnie's interest was now the high school, and sometimes church with Sister Carol, both of which she regarded in some subliminal way as the path to a final rich destination.

Chapter 31

Bonnie, Shirley, Joanne, Alice, Sally, and Mary Kay. The Green Dots.

Sally's father owned a gasoline distribution business. She could have been one of the popular girls, living on the west side, but she was too bossy and an all 'A' student. Brainy girls were always suspect. In addition to having a nice house, her family had a summer cottage at a nearby lake. There is a blurry picture of Bonnie, Sally, Joanne, and Shirley in a rowboat at that lake. It isn't clear, but Bonnie can make herself out, leaning over the side of the boat, dipping one hand into the water.

Once the girls stayed there overnight without Sally's parents. Sally had a bottle of whiskey and they all tried it and became quite drunk. They sang their school song raucously and wandered outside of the cabin for a while, hoping to attract some boys at another cottage across the lake. There were a few answering hoots and hollers. Sound carried easily over water, but that was as far as it went. Bonnie took nothing from the cottage. She had almost given up her habit of stealing small trinkets, realizing it served no purpose and it no longer excited her. The next item she took would have to be helpful to her plan of being rich. The clear path had not yet revealed itself.

Mary Kay, an all 'A' student with thick-lensed glasses, was another social outcast. The Green Dots had invited her to be part of their little group. Her house was near another small lake that froze over in winter. Mary Kay's mother often played hostess after skating parties, serving toasted cheese sandwiches and chili. Mary Kay was the smartest and could be relied on when the others' assignments were unfinished.

A lot of quick copying went on in the school basement locker area. Bonnie wondered whether the teachers had a clue about this daily ritual cheating,

Always trying to be noticed by the boys, the Green Dots' loud greetings to one another continued at the roller rink, located on the far south side. It was a popular gathering place. Bonnie still loved to roller skate, and wishfully recalled her friend, Rita, at times. *Rita could be trusted*, she thought. *I loved Rita.*

Bonnie skated gracefully around the floor's circle, sometimes skating backwards, showing off her curvy figure. Her breasts, now fully developed bounced up and down as she moved. She heard a boy whisper "Boomity, boom," as she skated near him. She considered it an honor. That's what they called Shelly, the big breasted blonde, junior girl who all the Green Dots envied.

Bonnie enjoyed her soft fullness and the way her bra, now a Coleman's Department Store bra, lifted them to compelling points. She knew if she played her cards right this would be of help in getting her the riches she desired. Some of the boys had pin-up posters of Betty Grable and Rita Hayworth in their lockers, displaying their enticing cleavage. Bonnie was proud of her generous proportions—a size 34C! She could hear the guys whisper as she walked by. She was almost a match for Shelley.

However, that spring of Bonnie's sophomore year and the following summer brought on an unhappy turn of events A boy and a girl were to be chosen for a six-week scholarship to Interlochen, a famous music camp in the lower peninsula of Michigan. Bonnie had never been to the Lower Peninsula, let alone a music camp, and it was free. She still worked faithfully on her piano skills and was the accompanist not only for the orchestra, but also for the chorus. She knew she was the best and had expectations of being the chosen girl. She still sang in the girl's trio begun in junior high.

Now the trio wore matching off-the-shoulder pink pique dresses During all-school assemblies they sang popular songs which had been arranged for them by Daddy. Slow *Boat to China* was their favorite. Once, while singing *Smoke Gets in Your Eyes,* one of the spotlights exploded, filling the auditorium with a smoky haze, and the whole assembly laughed. That was disconcerting, but the girls soldiered on, not missing one note.

The trio volunteered to sing at the Veteran's Hospital and the County Poor House on the outskirts of town where old people lived who had no family to care for them, or who didn't wish to care for them. T0ese people just sat there with heads drooped onto their chests, sometimes shaking back and forth.

Bonnie was put off by the fetid smell and orangey lighting in the Poor House. Those audiences never responded to their singing with a smile or applause. That was okay, because points were awarded to Bonnie in the Community Outreach program sponsored by the high school student council.

At the Spring all school assembly, Joanne, still singing off key, was announced as the winner of the scholarship. Bonnie was wracked with jealousy and anger and felt weakened, betrayed by Joanne, who had the popular twin cheerleading cousins and was an only daughter in a home that gave her every advantage they possibly could.

Joanne was even included in popular kids' activities, like being asked to help with decorations in the school gym for the Sadie Hawkins dances or the Sock Hops. Bonnie watched, jealous, as Joanne began to flit around with a self-satisfied smirk, even when she was with the Green Dots. She no longer shared boy secrets with Bonnie in their telephone planning conversations.

Bonnie recalled the time in sixth grade when her shoe was hidden after gym class and she was locked in the shower room. Joanne had been part of the plot, she felt sure, as she had seen her join the others sidelong smiles with that same little smirk. This was the person she now wanted to take something from, something important, something world shattering. She resolved to bide her time for the moment of retribution she felt was sure to come.

Chapter 32

"Let's go over the seven deadly sins" said Sister Carol.

"Yes, Sister, I know what they are," Bonnie blubbered through tears, "Pride, envy, hatred, idolatry, lust, anger, and gluttony" She had run to the convent instead of the ski hill after school that Friday.

"Sister, I'm not chosen for the Interlochen scholarship. It's so unfair. Why Joanne? You know she plays poorly and sings out of tune."

"Bonnie, it takes longer for a singer to mature. She's been faithful to her lessons and you've become a little spotty in attendance."

"But Sister,…"

"Now calm down, Bonnie. Think over the sins you've just named. Shall we point to anger and envy? These feelings can make you sick, and, more importantly put your immortal soul in danger. Here's your chance to exercise the virtue of humility. Now, Joanne needs to prepare a piece for the summer camp. She's working on a song that Mr. Beaverson wants her to sing for the next school assembly. I'd like you to accompany her."

Sister Carol opened a drawer in the music cabinet, took out a piece and handed it to Bonnie. *Songs My Mother Taught Me* was the title. The title swam before her eyes. That song, again! Had there been no advancement in her repertoire?

"I just can't, Sister," she cried even more loudly, tears coming faster and faster, her snot running down over her mouth.

"Yes, you can and will. Humility, Bonnie, humility. You'll not make a good nun unless you practice this virtue constantly. Besides, when you enter the convent after graduation, you will have so many opportunities to use your musical skills. Your talent was God-given, and He will be the director of the path you must take. You would do well to look at the lives of the holy martyrs. That will be of help to you on your own path."

The martyrs? Bonnie fumed inwardly as she left Sister Carol. She remembered the scrapbook she had kept of the pictures of martyrs and their fates. They were burned, stoned, pierced with arrows—even crucified like Jesus. She was still fascinated, by the picture of St. Agnes. Was she beheaded? She couldn't remember. They always called out her name during the Mass, when the saints were listed. St. Agnes was pure. The story said she was paraded through the street naked, covered only by her long flowing hair. She had refused to give up her virginity.

Nor will I, Bonnie thought, *but I'll never, never be a nun.* "Damn Joanne and damn Sister Carol" she swore aloud as she headed for home.

She didn't sleep that night. The next morning, Saturday, she got up before sunrise, dressed quickly, and headed down the twenty-six steps. She didn't know where she was going, but just had to go somewhere. The ice truck was stopped in front of the Bruno's. She hopped onto the tailgate and hung on tight, her hands, without mittens, stuck to the metal. The truck headed east on Margaret Street. It didn't stop until it reached the ice house, a low wooden, open structure on the shore of Lake Wakesha. Cut from the frozen lake, the house held large blocks of ice covered with sawdust.

She jumped down from the tailgate, tearing some skin from her hands, and continued walking along the shore for another ten minutes. The sun was rising by this time. Finally, exhausted, she sat on a large flat rock on the shore near the deepest part of the lake. The rock was big enough for her to lie back. This was the forbidden part of the lake for swimming. Some people had even drowned in its deep water.

It was cold on the rock, but she didn't care. She had been inured to cold as a child, swimming in the icy waters of Lake Superior. Cold and water were her friends.

As she gazed up at the early morning dark blue sky, she watched a long, narrow, densely composed cloud making its way from west to east. *On its journey*, she thought. *Just like me.*

Exploring. She felt a kinship with the cloud. No stopping it. When it was finally out of sight, a sense of peace washed over her as a flock of black winter birds came into sight. She resolved with a renewed certainty that her moment of triumph would come.

Chapter 33

Junior proms, senior hops, Bonnie went to everyone, being more careful to pick the escort she wanted. No more Bobby Romonogli. They would have to be from the east or west side.

Ron Tomaso had started to hang around her locker when she was getting books for class. One day, after school, he asked her to go to a movie, an official date. His father owned the local bowling lanes and evidently fared well enough to be able to live on the east side, even though they were originally Italians from the north side. Ron's mother sponsored the teas for the ladies' music club.

Bonnie had learned to turn on what she called "my shine" around some of the boys who interested her. It was a feeling that raced through her body, giving the victim of the shine the hope that he would be able to go a little far with her.

The underground song, sung to the tune of *Bye, Bye, Black Bird* instead used the words, *Bye, Bye, Cherry*. Bonnie had a good idea of what that meant, thanks to the special girls-only class about reproduction. She renewed her decision to keep that mysterious cherry intact. This was a prize which she would hang onto, despite her yearnings for something more than the furtive kisses and embraces in parked cars.

She went to the movie with Ron. Ron drove his father's car, a blue Ford. He hadn't picked her up at the door, just tooted his horn instead of walking up the steps. It didn't matter because her parents were out. Annie laughingly wished her good luck with this one when she heard the horn's beep-beep. They stopped at his home to meet his parents. Bonnie felt awkward in their presence. They were so formal and never smiled. Mr. Tomaso was bald and stern looking. *Ron looks like him*, she thought, *except he has hair.* It was a quick in-and-out visit. Ron was sixteen, like Bonnie, and he had recently gotten his driver's license. *He drives like an old man*, thought Bonnie.

They sat near the front row in the theater, in the center, so they had to climb over a few people. Bonnie couldn't remember what the movie was, but she did remember Ron reaching for her hand and holding it the entire time. His hand was a mass of sweat and she was repelled, but she didn't pull away. There was no kiss when he dropped her off at the bakery.

She went to the prom that year with Ronnie in another borrowed dress. He gave her an orchid corsage for her wrist. The after party was at the Riverside Club. She let him kiss her a few times, sticking to the plan offered by Sister Carol—nothing below the neck. After he dropped her off, she ran up the twenty-six steps, tripping once on the hem of her gown. She put the orchid on the top shelf of the refrigerator.

Her mother, impressed that her date was wealthy, was waiting for her when she got home and wanted to know every detail from the evening. "Oh, oh," her mother went on and on, "this is so exciting, an east side boy. Your orchid will keep for many days in the refrigerator. They've come all the way from Hawaii I've been told."

Bonnie took the corsage out for the next few days trying to get a sweet scent, thinking there would be a perfume from that faraway island, but there was no discernable odor, just an unpleasant smell like the flowers she had thrown away from the altar vases when she had helped Sister Carol in the church chancel.

Her last date with Ronnie was for the sophomore school picnic at a local park. Ron had served his purpose, and sensing Bonnie's reluctant response to his feeble advances, did not ask her out again.

Bonnie was beginning to flirt more, and had no trouble getting Friday night dates. The class picture in her junior year, shows a more presentable image, hair long and wavy—the waves were natural, she had discovered, when Carla's perm finally grew out. Beer and vinegar rinses gave it a softer look. In the picture, she is wearing a scooped neck sweater and a choker with a cameo pinned at the center. It is her mother's cameo. She is still standing in the back row, so only the top part of her bodice shows.

During the previous summer, since turning sixteen, she had managed to get a job as a car hop at the local root beer stand, just a block west of Margaret Street and across Highway 141. Bonnie could afford to buy her own clothes now, pencil skirts, angora sweaters, penny loafers, and saddle shoes. She loved shoes even though the shoe store didn't carry her size. Her feet had grown long and narrow. She managed to squeeze into a size nine.

Her boss, Mr. Simpson, at the root beer stand was another pincher, always looking so smiley and jolly, furtively having his way with any of the girls who were unfortunate enough to have to go inside the serving stand to wash the beer mugs. *Hello, Jolly, Jolly, goodbye, Tolly, Tolly*, she thought.

She'd said farewell to the bakery job when she took the car hop one. She was paid in checks, not cash. Small checks, but she knew who the best tippers were. All the girls did. "Here comes Mr. Five Cent, your turn to get his root beer." The girls made sure to take their place in line for the nicest patrons, who left dimes and even quarters.

The biggest crowds on the lot came after nine o'clock, on Saturdays, after the seven o'clock movie ended. The cars piled in at every angle, many carrying snuggling couples, but also a lot of single guys slumped in their driver's seat, elbows resting on the open driver door window. It looked like they might fall out of the vehicle. They were good tippers.

The war had ended and just about everyone was getting a new car—mostly Fords. All the Green Dots' dads had new cars. Not Father, though. He still tootled around in the Model A. Bonnie drove it, too, since she had passed her driver's test, even being able to use the choke when starting the engine and expertly managing the floor shift on the steepest hills.

The root beer stand was where Bonnie first heard strings of bad words coming from Nell Sparpani, a northsider. Nell was an independent sort, with a pugnacious don't care attitude. Fucks, shits, and assholes streamed regularly from her bright red lip-sticked mouth. Bonnie both admired and feared her. Alice said Nell had "done it!" Mr. Simpson never asked Nell to help with the wash-ups.

Sometimes on weekends, she, Nell, and Corky—another car-hop—went with a few of the guys after closing time to Lake Wakesha, where they chug-a-lugged beer on the beach, then ran fully clothed into the lake, grabbing on to each other in any possible way. Someone always tried for Bonnie's breasts and came close at times, but she was careful to evade them in a laughing, teasing way—all promise, but no fulfillment. She had become an expert.

Joanne confessed to Bonnie that she liked a senior, Tom Jones. "He's so cute, humm," she said.

"I know who you mean, Joanne, but he's a senior. He's too old for you. Forget it. Aren't you going with Bob Dunmar?"

"He's a sort of bore. I'm going to try for Tom Jones, anyway. My cousin said he's a great dancer, humm."

The root beer stand was where Bonnie met Tom Jones one evening in August. He was going to graduate in the middle of the year and planned to enlist into the army. He was cute and Bonnie fell hard for him. He asked her for a date one night when he drove in for a root beer. On their many dates, he did manage to get below the neck, but not below the waist. Just a venial sin, she decided.

Tom was a west side boy, red-haired, freckled, a little moon-faced; he was a star basketball player. He often played in pick-up games and liked to show off as he stomped down the court, dribbling, dodging, dribbling, passing the ball, getting it near the basket and dunking it in, then repeating the whole process over and over again. *So loud*, Bonnie thought. The referee's whistle, the yelling among the players. She didn't enjoy watching, but she played the part of the adoring fan.

Tom's father, in a wheel chair, was blind in one eye. His hair was a faded red, an older image of Tom. Tom's younger sister, Louise, was all red and freckled, too. She was a freshman at the high school and belonged to a popular crowd who had been together since kindergarten. Their house was well appointed, but on the dark side. They had a live-in housekeeper. Tom said his father had been injured in a mining accident and had received a large settlement from the mining company.

His mother had died in childbirth while giving birth to Louise. The housekeeper, Audra, was so solicitous of Mr. Jones that Bonnie immediately understood that she was more than a housekeeper.

"Here's Bonnie, Al. Isn't she a pretty one," Audra murmured, talking close to Mr. Jones ear as if he were deaf as well as partially blind. Then she took his hand and gave it a squeeze.

"Have a nice time, you two," said Mr. Jones acknowledging the squeeze by putting his other hand over Audra's in a fond manner.

We'd better get going, Bonnie, said Tom. "We'll be late for the movie." He said "Goodbye" to his dad, but not to Audra.

Snow came early that year. By October the kids were back on the ski hill. Tom was a good skier. Instead of the walk to the hill, he drove Bonnie after school in his two-seater coupe, which had a rumble seat. Sometimes Joanne grumpily rode the rumble seat, much to Bonnie's satisfaction. It was cold back there when the wind was blowing. Bonnie and Joanne remained friends but it wasn't as close as it had been. Bonnie could feel the ties breaking in a sad way.

The Jones belonged to the country club, and Tom asked Bonnie to the annual fall dance. *A step up at last*, thought Bonnie. One of the other Green Dots, Shirley went too, but her date was her brother. Bob Dunmar was there with another girl. Joanne wasn't asked. Mary Kay and Alice were not permitted to date.

For this occasion, Bonnie bought her own new dress, a yellow strapless gown, made by a seamstress on the southside of town, who had a dress shop on her enclosed front porch. *Another Carla*, Bonnie thought, *making dresses instead of setting perms*.

There were so many curious places in Copper Ridge. There was a green painted house, almost hidden behind the post office, a smaller version of the Green Garage, Boys were seen lining up there regularly to get their "introduction to life," Sally said, though Bonnie had never witnessed this lineup.

She thought she recognized one of the ladies from the closed Tramontine store on Margaret Street, but she wasn't sure. The lady, thin and heavily rouged, was gaudily dressed for Copper Ridge during the day, more like a dress she had seen worn in pictures of city dance halls. She moved quickly and kept her eyes lowered. Bonnie felt a little chill when she passed her in front of the J. C. Penny store.

The dance at the country club was a major affair. East and west side couples paraded about the dance floor. There was a sweet punch ladled from an intricately cut large glass bowl into smaller cut glass cups with tiny handles. *These are so awkward to hold*, Bonnie thought, but she managed as best she could, looking to see how the others did it with just a thumb and one finger.

The Sammy Tomasi Band provided the music, so Daddy was there at the baby grand piano looking as handsome as ever. He would give a sideways glance and little smile at the ladies who seemed always to be able to move their partners near the bandstand. He nodded one time at Bonnie. There was a subtle steamy air to the whole dimly lit setting. *Just another Al's Jukebox Joint*, Bonnie thought, *with a pretend air of respectably.*

Chapter 34

It wasn't yet Halloween, and there came more snow— deep, powdery, and cold. The skiing was great. The cold caused crystals to form on lashes and brows. Bonnie took several runs in her slow traverse across-the-hill fashion. The hill was lit every night until nine o'clock.

One night, after skiing, Tom drove her home and parked in front of the bakery, and in his usual fashion, worked his way down to her breasts, grabbing through the heavy ski jacket. "Let me go further," he begged. "Please, please, Bonnie, I love you so much." Bonnie wanted to satisfy him, but suddenly felt uncomfortable. She knew he wasn't the one.

"No, not now, Tom, not tonight," she said, though she meant not ever. She excused herself quickly, "My feet are freezing. I have to get my history assignment done." She felt so confused. She liked him— a lot—but had to get away, and she did.

The next day at school, she smiled and said "Hi, Tom" to him as she walked by his locker. He didn't respond. He didn't even look at her. He behaved as if he had never known her. Bonnie was crestfallen, but managed to compose herself as she met up with Mary Kay and Alice on the way to the first class.

"Finish the assignment?" Alice asked.

"Yes, I was up late, but it's done. Bonnie said glumly. She felt numb from Tom's rebuff, *I hate him*, she thought. It was a burning hatred, deep in her soul.

That December, Tom approached her after six weeks of the silent treatment. "Come with me to the Christmas dance at the club?" he asked, as if there had never been a silence between them.

"Gee, this is a surprise, Tom," she said. *He didn't know she hated him?*

"I was just testing you," he tried to explain. "I really love you Bonnie."

She noticed a little tag of skin alongside of his lower lip. *It's so ugly. Why haven't I seen this before?*

"Well, guess I passed your test then, eh? Sure, I'll go with you," she said brightly.

Tom was only a month from graduation and about to join the army. A lot of girls liked Tom, including Joanne, who had never been to a country club dance. Bonnie began to form the revenge plot. Since Joanne had gotten the music scholarship the summer before, she still felt the sting of that rejection. Now, with Tom, she had had a second rejection to add to it.

After the Christmas dance, and before he left for the army, Tom asked Bonnie if she loved him. "Of course, I do, Tom, I'll miss you so much," she said, turning on her best shine. In his first letter to her, he professed his love for her in flowery words. He wanted to marry her when he got out of the army in two years. She read the letter over the phone to Joanne.

"Tom Jones wants to marry me," Bonnie crowed.

"You're so lucky, Bonnie," said Joanne. "He's a great guy, humm."

"Well, I'm not going to accept," said Bonnie. "I don't love him the least little bit."

She saved the address but left the letter unanswered, not any of the next two either. Then the letters stopped. She burned each letter in her mother's oversized marbled ashtray with the cow-eared feet.

Bonnie shared the Tom story with Sister Carol, during one of her lessons.

"Good for you, Bonnie," she said, "but you should write and tell him you won't marry him, or he might keep his hopes up. He's serving our country and it's not right to keep him hanging. Marriage is not in the cards for you, Bonnie."

You'd never be happy as a married woman was Sister Carol's

continuous caution, still pressing for Bonnie to enter the convent after graduation. Suddenly she began to share a little of her past.

"Have courage," she said. "My own father disowned me when I entered the order, but I've never turned back. He's a prosperous shopkeeper in St. Louis. I was his only child, and he wanted me to take over the shop when he retired, but I heard the call and I responded. I became a Bride of Christ. Pray that you hear God's call. Don't turn a deaf ear. That's your only path to happiness."

Bonnie wondered about this call. Surely Sister Carol had had suitors. She was so pretty. Aloud she agreed with Sister, but kept her fingers crossed behind her back. Sister suddenly looked flustered by this personal sharing of her life with Bonnie. She gave a harrumph, cleared her throat, and turned abruptly to the lesson at hand.

"Now listen to this recording of the Debussy piece you're practicing," she said.

Bonnie listened as the pianist played *Claire de Lune* The recording was scratchy, but she became rapt with the beauty of the performance. Daddy liked this piece, too. It was the only classic he played. He had had to learn it, as it was the most often requested classical piece by patrons at the piano bar where he played on Wednesday nights. The bar was in the basement of the Combination Restaurant. The stairs leading down were outside. It had an iron rail, much like the iron rail on the first six bakery steps only leading down, not up. At night, an overhead street lamp enticingly lit them.

Bonnie thought there were a lot of possibly mortal sins going on down there. Fun sins probably. That was why Saturday's confession lines were so long. So far her sins were still venial, not going too far with her dates. Tom was the only one who had gone below the neck.

Bonnie and Daddy had taken different musical paths a few years before. Father wanted her to learn chords and jazz licks. Bonnie persisted in her love of the classics, largely due to Sister Carol. That was one battle Sister had won.

When she was seventeen, Daddy let her sing with the Tomasi Band as a featured vocalist at the Riverside Club for just a few sets. Bonnie thought she did a pretty good job, liking the mike, harkening back to her days at the radio station in Marquette where she sang her little songs on Saturday afternoons.

Bonnie loved the night club setting with its small intimate tables and red velvet covered chairs, the bandstand lit by a spotlight, the long gleaming bar in an adjoining room. She had had her sips of beer from Grandpa Smith's cup and whiskey at Sally's camp, but at the club, she was only allowed a soft drink between sets. Cream soda was still her favorite.

She watched the dating couples as they danced, holding each other closely, not like the school dances where a proper distance was required by the chaperoning faculty, who seemed to overlook the grip of Mr. Egizzi. She thought they felt sorry for him, being married to Mrs. Egizzi, who Joanne said was unable to give him a child. Mrs. Egizzi came to the school dances, too, and sat near the other faculty members. She always wore a blue dress, and her mannish, short cut hair was drugstore bleached blonde.

She recognized Mr. and Mrs. Bruno, her neighbors on Margaret Street. She smiled at them as they danced near the mike while she was singing and gave them a little wave, but there was no sign of recognition from them.

Who are these people? she thought, *with their new car every two years and an old grandfather living in one room of their house. He's just a car dealer, and she dresses up every day and gets dropped off by her husband for a stuck-up walk downtown past the five and dime, Primo's hat shop, and the Penny store. They're not rich, just pretenders. I'm not going to be like them.* She sang another number with the band during the next set, *Body and Soul.* She gave that torch song her all.

Chapter 35

Mr. Ginther came on to relieve Mr. Beaverson of his chorus duties as the marching band was taking so much of his time. Mr. Ginther dreamed of such great things. An operetta! HMS Pinafore. The chorus members were in an uproar because of the extra rehearsal schedule he posted on the hall bulletin board. Bonnie was the pianist again.

Most of the cast, including Joanne as Miss Buttercup, failed to appear for many of the rehearsals or straggled in late. The operetta was finally canceled and so was the annual spring choral concert as nothing was prepared. Mr. Ginther was let go at the end of the school year. People commented quietly that it was because he was Jewish, and not that there was no spring choral concert. There was an underlying prejudice in the east and west parts of town against anyone that wasn't Swedish or English. Italians, of course were suspect, too. The only Jewish family in town, the Golds, were tolerated because Mr. Gold was so generous in monetary contributions to the Band Parent organization.

Anna Gold, their daughter, who was in Bonnie's class, played the clarinet, and played it so well that she was always first chair in band and orchestra. She had few friends.

She was accused of cheating during the spring semester. Everyone cheated, notes written on palms for the quizzes, assignment papers copied, tests stolen from the principal's office. No one knew who Anna's accuser was or at least wouldn't name anyone.

Anna had to go to the dean's office after her name was called over the loud speaker. The Dean of Girls was Miss Helmer, a large grizzly woman who wore thick bottle bottom glasses, which enlarged her pupils to the size of the lens. She was a frightening figure. Anna was suspended for three days. "She cheats on everything" was the talk among the kids. Even the Green Dots commented on this, but it made Bonnie uncomfortable because she thought someone had told a lie about Anna's cheating. *Anna was smart. She didn't need to cheat*, she thought, but she didn't voice her opinion aloud. She feared rejection by the Green Dots because she felt somewhat of an outsider, too.

Anna's father owned the produce distribution center for the entire Upper Peninsula and even some of the neighboring territory of Northern Wisconsin. Their house was on the west side, quite removed from the other houses. There was an expansive lawn, and in summer, lovely flower gardens were planted in grey stone circles.

Bonnie made it a point to try to befriend Anna when she returned to school after the suspension. Anna was quiet, and seldom acknowledged Bonnie's overtures.

"Anna, I've brought my lunch today, Bonnie said, when she saw her standing forlornly by her locker. My mother packed an extra sandwich. How about sharing with me?"

"Oh, I'm not very hungry. Thanks, Bonnie. I had a big breakfast with my dad." Anna mumbled, her head down.

Bonnie tried other things like walking with her to their classroom or inviting her to the Green Dots' skating party at Mary Kay's house. Shirley joined Bonnie in the effort to make Anna feel welcome but their efforts were useless. Anna appeared to be beaten.

Her parents removed her from school and sent her to a private boarding school far away, Milwaukee, Bonnie heard. That was certainly far away. *Maybe I'll go there some day,* Bonnie thought. She yearned to escape the tedium of high school, and even the Green Dots.

There were no more donations from the Golds to the Band Parent organization, and the band had to forego the purchase of a new bass drum and new uniforms in the black-and-gold school colors that Mr. Beaverson had been promising the kids for years.

Chapter 36

Alfeo Strong's father owned the local foundry in Copper Ridge and three other foundries in Wisconsin. Alfeo had a sister, Jean, who was a senior. Jean wore the very best sweaters. She was tall blonde, slender, and graceful; she had been accepted at Smith College where all the girls wore plaid pleated skirts and white blouses. Their buttoned cashmere sweaters were worn like a cape, the body of the sweater down the back like a protective shield, with the sleeves perfectly placed, like a ladder over their breasts.

At least that was the picture Bonnie saw when she looked up Smith College in the library encyclopedia. Jean had had the lead in every school play. The Strongs were Copper Ridge's community leaders They kept aloof for the most part, but had one yearly party—the Strong Ball, not held at the country club, but at their home. It was the biggest house in Copper Ridge, located at the top of the East Side hill on 'C' street. That's how streets were named on the east side, by letters, A B, C, all the way up to G.

The Strong house was of grey stone, more like a castle really. It had two turrets and several chimneys that looked like turrets, and tall mullioned windows. The high double arched entrance door, before the circular drive, was inviting and forbidding at the same time.

Behind the house was a tennis court, a pool house and a kidney-shaped pool. *Why have a pool?* Bonnie thought. *It's so cold and snowy most of the year, only three short summer months,* but she liked the idea of having a pool, nonetheless.

Mr. Strong was the Upper Peninsula golf champion almost every year. He had well-muscled arms, which gave him an edge on the long drives, despite his otherwise short, pudgy stature. He liked to wear a long-billed baseball hat, and he had a toothpick always moving around in his mouth like it was attached to his tongue. Bonnie couldn't help staring at this phenomenon when she saw him occasionally on the northside, getting his favorite Italian foodstuffs at Crispigna's market.

Mrs. Strong was taller than her husband, as was their daughter, Jean. Mrs. Strong seldom appeared with her husband on the golf course, preferring to golf at the Lady's Day Tuesday tee-offs. She was slender, like Jean, smooth complexioned, her skin golden all over.

Mrs. Strong had grown up on the northside, where her immigrant Italian parents ran a small restaurant, famous for their spicy porketta sandwiches, served personally by her parents, Mr. and Mrs. Nannini. Mrs. Strong's dark hair was always worn in a thick French twist, a jeweled comb holding it in place. She had a striking, angular face and almond eyes, strangely blue.

Observing that northside girls and boys married east and west siders, Bonnie vowed she would marry Alfeo. She didn't have a game plan, but. what had been desultory now became a challenge.

One evening, Jean was crammed in the back seat of a car coming from the Riverside Club, where she had been at a pre-graduation party. The club was in Wisconsin, just across the border from Michigan. One had to enter Wisconsin over a long curving bridge, which spanned the Menominee River. The road passed the Green Door, on the Michigan side of U.S. Highway 141.

It was March, still snowy, and the roads were icy due to a recent daytime thaw that refroze at night. The crowded car was traveling at a high speed, driven by a popular boy named Cliff. It was Cliff's father's car, a Ford. The car began to skid on the bridge, and it hit the guard rail on the right side. The laughter stopped. Jean flew forward from the back seat straight through the front windshield. They said she was decapitated. Most everyone else suffered minor injuries. Cliff had both legs broken and he was in a cast for several weeks. Police found a whiskey bottle in the wreckage. Mrs. Strong canceled bridge club that week-end.

The whole student body was in shock. Fearful looks of disbelief filled the halls and classrooms on the following Monday. Teachers attempted to carry on their lectures and assignments in a subdued voice, knowing that no one thought it important. Nor did they.

Jean's funeral was to be on the following Wednesday, and an announcement was made over the loud speaker by Miss Helmer, saying there would be no school on that day for those students who wished to attend the service. The whole junior and senior class went, some even going to the wake at the Cross funeral home the night before. "I wonder if the casket will be open, given that her head was cut off," Bonnie overheard one of the boys say as she passed by a group of them gathered around Cliff's locker. At the funeral, Bonnie watched Mr. and Mrs. Strong holding their arms around Alfeo, sitting in the front pew of St. Joseph's church. Sister Carol was in the first pew, too.

They're Catholic, thought Bonnie. *So am I. I must find a way to meet Alfeo. I'm going to marry him. Maybe Sister Carol. No, not Sister Carol. She wants me to go to the convent. I will find a way. Maybe the spring play.* Joanne said Alfeo was going to try out for a part in memory of his sister, Jean.

"Where did you hear that, Joanne," asked Bonnie.

"My cousin, Barbarina, told me," said Joanne. "She's in one of Alfeo's classes. The play's director asked Alfeo if he would try out and he agreed, humm."

The spring play was to be a production of *Junior Miss*. Bonnie wanted to be in this play since it wasn't a musical and she wouldn't have to play the piano. There was a lot of buzz about who would be in cast, as Jean Strong would no longer be a contender. Bonnie talked it over with the Green Dots, and they urged her to try for a part. Bonnie was active in the speech and debate club and had been awarded a first prize in the fall speech competition with three other schools in the Upper Peninsula.

She recited from an essay by John Donne called *No Man Is an Island*. She spent long hours memorizing the two-page piece while pacing around the kitchen linoleum floor.

"Shut up, will you, Bonnie. I can't concentrate," Alan shouted from the front room. "I'm trying to read. No one can do anything around here, what with Daddy's piano pounding and now this incessant reciting. You either know it or you don't."

"You're not very encouraging," Bonnie would yell back, then had to begin again from the top, having lost her train of thought during the exchange. *That's Alan*, Bonnie thought, *always with his nose in a book*.

Bonnie's skin was now clear and glowing after a small bout of acne the year before. She only had to squeeze out the occasional black head. She followed Daddy's tip on how to let soap foam dry on her face like a mask, then wash it with cold water. Before heading off to school, she repeated this process at least three times every morning. Her mother stressed the importance of using cold cream every night to remove every bit of make-up. Her mother certainly had creamy skin despite her expanding plumpness and Daddy was still a handsome man.

Sally often said, and the Green Dots agreed, "You have the best-looking Dad."

At the last minute, Joanne said she might as well try out for a part, too.

"It's not a musical, Joanne," Bonnie pointed out. "There's no singing in this one and you've never taken part in the speech or drama club."

"Okay, Bonnie, you're right, and I've never tried acting anyway, humm"

That was true. Her speaking voice was monotonous, and she had that self-important slight smacking twitch of her lips following the pursed lip humm at the end of sentences when reciting a poem in English class or just plain talking about anything. Bonnie felt satisfied that she had convinced Joanne not to try out for a role.

At the tryout Bonnie was a little nervous, but quickly settled down after she began reading a part with the gorgeous Alfeo. The tryouts were after school at three o'clock. Mr. Alquist was the Drama Club advisor, and he knew, unlike poor Mr. Ginther, that the kids wanted to be out by four so they would still have time on the ski hill. It was spring and some of the snow had already started to melt, but the upper hill was still packed hard, though snow was starting to rot underneath in places near the bottom.

Shortly before four, Joanne walked in, accompanied by the twin cheerleading cousins, Barbarina and Christina, and announced her desire to read for a part. She wore a dress made for her by the local dressmaker, copied from a picture of a dress in *Seventeen Magazine,* that she casually mentioned before she started reading.

She got one of the roles, along with another popular girl, Lynn. Alfeo got a small part, too. Mr. Alquist said it would be good for him, as he had been downcast since his sister's death. Mr. Alquist said there would be a memoriam for Jean printed in the play's program.

Bonnie wasn't even cast as the mother, though she was tall enough, and loud enough, and her hair, now lightened, was long, and she walked so straight, as her mother had made her practice many times, walking around the kitchen floor with a heavy book balanced on her head.

I'm so jealous it's making me sick, she thought. Now she truly hated Joanne, the betrayer, but she pretended to be happy for her. She didn't sleep for many nights, in her sick envy, saying her rosary over and over without the beads, ticking out the Hail Marys on her fingers as she lay there next to Annie. Jealousy, one of the seven deadly sins. This one was mortal, and she would probably get a longer penance when she confessed on the next Saturday.

Alfeo took Joanne to the prom. Bonnie went with Dan Ceresoli.

Chapter 37

Junior year seemed frantic at times to Bonnie. The jammed lockers, books, notebooks, classes, teachers, tests, stairways, long halls, proms, hops, assemblies, football games, basketball games, orchestra concerts and chorus concerts made each semester pass quickly.

The special concerts stood out—the Community Concert Series. They were the real events— not presented by amateurs, but by recognized artists, some from New York City! That series was for the adults. Students chosen by Mr. Beaverson did the ushering. He saw to it that Bonnie was picked as an usher. After everyone was seated, the ushers got to sit in the very front row, to the far-right side. There they sighed over the handsome guys from visiting college choirs and tried, sometimes helplessly to suppress many quiet giggles. Alice was chosen as an usher, too.

One performance featured a famous opera singer from the Metropolitan Opera, Blanche Thebom. She stood there on the stage unmoving while she sang songs in other languages. She looked beautiful, almost mesmerizing with her calm poise. She stood in the crook of the grand piano, one hand resting on the piano itself. She gave the tiniest nod to the pianist to begin the introductions to her songs.

After that concert, the ushers were permitted into the back-stage area in to have their programs signed by the star. Up close, Bonnie observed that the singer was thickly made-up, full dark red lips, black brows, long black false lashes, and heavily rouged cheeks. *Sort of like the ladies from the small green house where the boys lined up*, she thought. Bonnie felt shy as she asked Madam Thebom for her autograph. The pianist, who wore formal tails, stood a bit farther back. No one asked for his autograph. He wasn't the important one, *like me*, Bonnie thought.

A violinist all the way from Paris, France, was one of the performers on another evening. The pianist needed a page-turner and Mr. Beaverson chose Bonnie for the task. She was excused from afternoon classes to rehearse with them. She sat in a small chair at the left side of the piano bench. There she kept her eyes fixed on the complicated music, standing at the right moment, reaching for the right-hand page, and quickly turning it over, smoothing it flat down with a fast swipe over the new page so it didn't turn back to the previous page. She was so good at reading the music dots that she seldom needed a nod from the pianist which meant, *turn now*. She was that quick.

"What will you wear this evening?" he asked in a thick French accent. "It must be a nice gown."

She borrowed a dress from Mary Kay, again pink, the same one she had worn to the last prom. She felt beautiful that evening. The violinist played absolutely in tune. She hoped Alice would take note. He bowed deeply after each number. They were long pieces, one went on for almost a half hour. He turned to the pianist during the applause after each number, who stood briefly and bowed, too, though not as deeply, just a little nod. Bonnie did not get to bow, which was just as well as the lights made her feel all sweaty and even a little faint.

The Strongs didn't attend these concerts, though they did contribute to the expenses and their name was first in the program list of local supporters. Alfeo didn't come either. *Concerts are not the place to meet him*, Bonnie decided. She was jolted out of her musings when an announcement blared over the loud speaker. There was one in every classroom. Kids said it worked both ways, so the principal could listen to any classroom at any time.

"Bonnie Smith, come to the office, please." The voice boomed.

Now what? she thought. She hoped Alfeo had heard her name and would remember her from the play tryouts. This wasn't the first time she had been called. Usually it was to be questioned about Annie. Why wasn't she in school? Annie and the fast crowd often skipped school for an afternoon, or sometimes for the entire day.

Bonnie would offer some lame excuse to the dean like "She was sick this morning," or "My mother had to take her to the dentist." This excuse made her smile inside, as her mother didn't drive, but she hated having to go through the same pathetic drill. She knew the truant officer would have already picked Annie up. Miss Helmer glared through her thick lenses, her mouth pursed, when Bonnie entered, making her feel as though she was the guilty one for skipping school.

"Tell your father about this," the drill always ended. "Annie will be suspended for the next three days." *Why isn't Annie here taking the blame?* Bonnie thought. *Annie loves the suspensions. She's off somewhere having a good old time with her gang of miscreants. I'd like to be having fun, too, but I just don't fit in with that crowd.* She waited with dread for another onslaught of accusations.

To her surprise, she was invited to sit down. "I see you're in the college preparatory courses," began Miss Helmer. "Why is that?"

"My piano teacher, Sister Carol, insisted on that route, and she and my father agreed it was the best way to go, given my good grades."

"Your father, I understand, no longer works at the glider plant since it closed after the war."

That's true, Bonnie thought, *but he's a smart man.* He had never graduated from high school, having had to quit at age sixteen to work at the Piqua to help Grandma and Grandpa Smith buy groceries. She didn't volunteer this aloud, not wanting to get into an argument with scary Miss Helmer.

"He works at a woodworking plant, and he plays piano at different places almost every night," she responded. *What was this about anyway?* she wondered. "My mother works, too," she added, "at a restaurant, as a cook."

"Well, you should be taking typing and bookkeeping so you can get a job after graduation," said Miss Helmer. "You should be in the business courses. Latin and Spanish won't help you there. But I suppose it's too late now. Your family will never be able to afford college for you, or your sister and brothers." *Ha, there was no question about Annie ever being college material*, thought Bonnie

Bonnie had wondered about the college thing. The other Green

Dots were gone all one morning taking some sort of test to which she wasn't invited. "The college prep kids are taking a college entrance placement exam," Alice told her. "All of the National Honor Society kids have to take the test."

That was another hard knock for Bonnie. She was an all 'A' student, except for chemistry, the wax clogged sink insuring her 'B-'. She wanted to lash out in protest, but held her peace, as it wasn't Alice's fault. Nice Alice. A battle against this unfairness churned within her.

She looked around Miss Helmer's office and noticed an oil painting of Jean Strong. Miss Helmer saw her gaze. "Mr. and Mrs. Strong presented this painting along with a large contribution to the Drama Club," she said.

Well, good for them, Bonnie thought, *but they still have the handsome Alfeo and all that money. I'm going to have him and the money, too, somehow.*

"Mrs. Strong hasn't been well," Miss Helmer began. "She wants one of our students to come after school and drive her daily to the cemetery. I know you have your driver's license and can use the money. You'll be paid three dollars every day. She'll want someone on weekends, too. Mr. Strong is away a lot. And, from what I've gathered, she wants a sort of companion. Someone young, someone near her daughter Jean's age."

Yes, yes, thought Bonnie. *A perfect job. Goodbye to skiing and freezing feet, goodbye to early morning stints at the convent, playing that horrible electric keyboard, goodbye to the Christmas seasonal job, clerking at the five and dime sock counter, looking out of the front window and seeing Mrs. Bruno prance by in her latest hat from Primo's hat shop.*

She felt herself beginning to drift upward, like she did on the grounds of the school corner in Crystal Falls. She felt her world beginning to shift.

Alfeo, Alfeo, Alfeo. He'd been so quiet at school since the accident. He was tall, like Jean, and had his mother's dark hair and striking blue eyes. One eye, his left, had a lid that half covered the pupil, in a sort of permanent wink. It reminded her of her Grandmother Johnson's one glass eye look. Her eye that could see opened less than the glass eye. *It just makes Alfeo that much more attractive,* decided Bonnie.

Alfeo now avoided the popular kids, becoming something of a loner. Bonnie's brother, Alan, also a loner type, was often seen with Alfeo, even though Alan was three grades behind him in school. They traded books and often walked together to classes talking quietly, shoulder-to-shoulder, books in hand. Alfeo invited Alan to the country club on summer weekends and taught him to play golf. Alan used clubs provided by Alfeo. They were almost always doing something together.

This could only be good, Bonnie exalted to herself. Aloud she said, "Yes, Miss Helmer, thank you, Miss Helmer. When can I start the job?" She anticipated being around Alfeo and practicing her best shine whenever he was near. Even though Alfeo had gone to the prom with Joanne because of their being thrown together in the class play, it had only been that once and nothing came of it, though Joanne did her best to keep reminding the Green Dots of that supposed triumph.

"Did you meet his mother?" Sally asked Joanne.

"Well, no, she's been keeping to herself since the accident, but I know Alfeo likes me. It's just a matter of time before he asks me out again, humm" Joanne replied, importantly.

Bonnie's date at that same prom, Dan Ceresoli, another redhead, had been her fallback plan. His father owned a flower shop. He had provided the floral arrangements for Jean's funeral. The corsage Dan brought to her that evening—he even came to the door— was comprised of tiny yellow and pink tea roses. Bonnie thought it was pretty, but she didn't save it in the refrigerator.

Chapter 38

It would have to rain, Bonnie thought as she made her way up the hill on 'C' Street. *I'll get wet. I hope my soggy appearance doesn't lose me the job.* She ducked into the city library as the latest squall passed and checked out a new Perry Mason mystery for her mother. The prim librarian didn't want the book to get wet, so Bonnie waited until there was a lull in the rain, using the wait to check out the fairy tale section in the children's room. She hadn't read a fairy tale in so long. She lingered over the Grimm's section, wanting to find *East of the Sun and West of the Moon*, but she heard the rain stop its pattering on the windows and decided she had better move on. Another four blocks to the top of the hill in just the remaining drizzle, and there it was, the Strong castle.

Bonnie made her way to the back door where she noticed the pool overflowing from the downpour. The cook, Mrs. Prianti, let her in. She said she came every afternoon and prepared dinner for the Strongs. "Do you do the cleaning, too?" asked Bonnie.

"No that's Tolly's wife, Celia. She comes in every morning except Sundays to take care of the cleaning and the dirty dishes from the night before. The priest drives her up the hill after Mass, then he comes to pick her up around eleven o'clock, after lunch is laid out—leftovers from the last night's supper. Mrs. Strong never eats breakfast. Mr. Strong goes to the diner on Highway 141. It's the diner where the Greyhound bus stops. He always helps himself to several toothpicks at the cash register when he pays the bill. He never leaves a tip. At least that's what Pam the waitress told me."

So much information from one little question, thought Bonnie. She had hoped to hear her mention Alfeo. "Mrs. Strong is expecting you, Bonnie" Mrs. Prianti cut off further questioning, maybe thinking she had said too much. "She's in the library."

So, there was a library. Of course, there would be. It was a satisfying thought. "Go straight ahead through that door," Mrs. Prianti said. It was a swinging door. "The library is the third door on your left. Be sure to knock." Bonnie walked curiously down the long hall observing the family portraits. Alfeo and Jean were in several of them.

Reaching the library, she saw that the door was open. Seated in a green wing chair was Mrs Strong. She looked so different from what Bonnie was expecting. Her hair was pure white. Bonnie had heard of people whose hair had turned white from a scare. *Maybe grief does that too*, she thought. Mrs. Strong wore small reading glasses on the end of her nose.

Bonnie usually left her glasses off except when she was alone and needed to see small print, or when she drove Father's car. That was on her driver's license, on the back, stamped, *glasses required.*

"Hello Mrs. Strong," Bonnie said shyly, "I'm Bonnie Smith. Miss Helmer said you wanted me to come here after school."

Mrs. Strong looked at her for the longest time before saying anything, then stood and tucked her glasses into the pocket of the grey silvery gown she was wearing. Bonnie saw then that she was beautiful, even with her snow-white hair.

"I was told that you drive. I'm afraid I've never learned. I'd like to visit Jean's grave in the afternoons, and I'd expect you to drive me."

"Yes, of course," Bonnie answered in a small voice, as her eyes quickly darted around the large room taking in the tall book shelves on all three sides. This wasn't Grandma Smith's four short bookshelves holding books with mostly broken bindings. There were no books at Bonnie's house except for the ones Alan kept and the novels Bonnie brought her mother from the local library. And the hidden magazines, of course.

"You're all wet," Mrs. Strong said. "I'll have to find you a rain jacket. Are you afraid to drive in the rain?" It had started another downpour.

"No, Mrs. Strong. I'm used to the weather. I drive on icy days, too."

"Here, put this on." Mrs. Strong took a light green slicker from the hall closet near the front door. "It was Jean's," she said wistfully.

Bonnie knew that. She had seen Jean wearing it at football games. It fit Bonnie perfectly.

"Well then, the garage is this way." They went out the main entrance to the garage, which was just to the right of the castle. It looked like part of the house, the same stone; even the windows matched the rest of the house.

Bonnie pulled up on the handle at the bottom of the garage door and it slid up easily. The space revealed room for as many as three cars, but only one was there, a Buick. It was the only Buick she had seen in Copper Ridge. It looked brand new.

Mrs. Strong got into the front seat and Bonnie got behind the wheel. She had to take her glasses out of her skirt pocket. "Jean had to wear glasses when she drove, too," said Mrs. Strong.

A wave of happiness washed over Bonnie on hearing that Mrs. Strong was comparing her to Jean. It didn't last long. She looked in a panic for the stick shift on the floor, then realized it was on the steering wheel shaft, like the car she rode in with Tom Jones when they were dating.

Mrs. Strong handed her a key and Bonnie, filled with a false self-confidence, started the car, and backed it out onto the circular drive. It was an automatic shift, so easy. She felt better as she headed for the cemetery, at the very bottom of the hill and to the left on Highway 141, a little farther south near the veteran's hospital where she had entertained the sick soldiers as part of the girl's trio sing-outs. *I know every corner of this town*, she thought.

She had hoped to see Alfeo. Mrs. Strong mentioned in passing that he was at the foundry with his Dad, learning the ins and outs of the business. "He'll oversee everything one day," she said. "It's a lot to learn." *I'll be patient*, Bonnie thought. *Now that my world has shifted, it won't be long before I meet Alfeo.*

When they returned from the cemetery, Mrs. Strong said she hoped Bonnie would continue to come every afternoon.

"Yes, Mrs. Strong, I'd very much like to."

"Thank you, Bonnie. I think we're going to get along well. I'll look for you tomorrow then. You can keep the raincoat. It's still raining. I don't want you to catch cold, she said solicitously. Mr. Strong will have a check for you at the end of the week.

Bonnie left through the back door. There was a path along the top of the hill behind the Strong house. Bonnie knew of this path because Daddy had taken her there on blueberry picking expeditions. *Blueberry Hill*, he called it, like the song, then he would laugh. The path led to the northside of Copper Ridge.

Now I'm finally on the right path, she though, smiling. The Green Dots began to regard her with expectant looks, waiting for her to speak about her new job. Even Joanne, who had had that one date with Alfeo, had never been inside the Strong castle and had never met Mrs. Strong. She clung to Bonnie's arm in the friendliest way.

Bonnie's lips remained mum when the Strongs came up in conversation, immediately changing the subject to what movie was showing or the latest couplings at school. *Nothing is going to divert me from my plan to marry Alfeo*, she thought. *No one knows about my longing for a better life*. Bonnie was certain that expressing this desire aloud would be bad luck. Even Sister Carol, who still talked about the comforts and joys of convent life, was kept in the dark.

Sister Carol knew of Bonnie's new job with Mrs. Strong and expressed her sadness at the loss of beautiful Jean. "Mrs. Strong doesn't come to morning Mass anymore." She lamented. "She refuses to see Father when he calls. Is Mr. Strong still gone a lot on business?" How often do you go there?"

Questions, questions.

Bonnie's answers were polite, but non-committal. "I'm pretty busy with the chorus and orchestra stuff at school and haven't paid much attention to the Strong goings-on. I just do whatever little things Mrs. Strong asks."

She drew a mental circle around herself whenever the subject of the Strongs arose, like a moat around a castle, with a bridge that *would not come down*.

The reality was, Bonnie had never met Mr. Strong, who returned home—when he did return—after Bonnie left. Alfeo was absent, too, at the foundry or on the golf course or pool hall with her brother, Alan.

Bonnie couldn't understand Alfeo's desire to be with Alan. He was three years behind Alfeo in school, but having skipped two grades was now in the same class as Gus. *Still, he's smart*, she thought, *and loves to read. Maybe that's what Alfeo was looking for in a friend since the death of his sister. Someone to look out for.* It was a puzzle.

Alan didn't tease her as much as he used to, but there were still loud confrontations with Father. She asked Alan about Alfeo. What did they talk about? What did he like to do? She was full of questions, too, like Sister Carol.

"We talk about politics mostly. He said his mother wants him to be mayor of Copper Ridge someday."

"After college?" Bonnie asked.

"He's not going to college. His dad wants him to go right into the business. Alfeo worries about his mother," Alan replied, dismissively.

"Does he know I'm helping her out after school?" Bonnie would not let the topic of Alfeo go.

"Probably. He knows someone's there. Haven't you run into him?" asked Alan.

"No, there's just me and Mrs. Strong," That was as much as Bonnie could get out of Alan. He was tight-lipped, too.

Sister Carol commented on Bonnie's sweater one day. "It looks just like one Jean wore." It was Jean's. Mrs. Strong had insisted that Bonnie have it. It was sort of spooky, really. Mrs. Strong's name was Rosalie. She wanted Bonnie to call her that, as Jean used to do. "You remind me so much of my Jean," she'd say.

They had stopped the daily runs to the cemetery. Rosalie now wanted Bonnie to read to her or have cocoa and cookies in the kitchen, or play for her on their grand piano in the music parlor. "Jean played," she said. "She'd be as good as you if she had kept up her lessons with Sister Carol."

Bonnie felt she was becoming Jean in Mrs. Strong's eyes. It was confusing. She didn't want to be Alfeo's sister.

In social studies class, she managed to sit next to Alfeo in the double seating desks. Alfeo had to make up that class to graduate in June. So close. He hardly noticed her, but she noticed him, every little detail, even the small bit of unwashed dirt in his ear shell.

Bonnie kept that detail from the Green Dots. In their less-frequent get-togethers, the gossip always revolved around the same boring breakups and new couplings, that Bonnie had begun to find tedious, now that she was fixed on Alfeo. "I'll marry for love," Joanne said one day, when they were gathered at the Combination Diner, eating chili dogs. She was currently involved with a minor-league baseball player who frequented the town when his team was playing in the Upper Peninsula.

That's stupid, Bonnie thought, though she didn't say it aloud. Bonnie thought about how it was between her parents. They had married for love, and now there didn't seem to be any love lost between them. "Never marry a musician," her mother's mantra ran through her head. "I should have listened to your Grandma Johnson."

Joanne's parents, her silent father, filling in the circles in the daily newspaper, and her mother putting up the sauces and lentil soups and scrubbing the venetian blind slats, were no lovebirds either

Shirley's parents. They were never in the same room together. Sometimes when Bonnie came to call on Shirley, Shirley would still be in bed with her father. She adored her father. "Shirley, get up," her mother would call. "Bonnie's here." Shirley would appear, still in pajamas, a sheepish look on her face. *No, I won't marry for love*, Bonnie thought.

"Sorry, I have to leave for home," Bonnie said, ending the current discussion. "We're expecting company from out of town."

Grandma Johnson's sister, Great Aunt Lyda, was coming for a visit, all the way from Negaunee. Uncle Lemmy, Mother's brother was going to drive her. Without Violet, of course. Bonnie, Alan, Gus, and Annie sat on the first six cement steps waiting for the car to arrive

"Hi, Auntie," said Bonnie. *She looks so old*, Bonnie thought.

"Come and give Auntie a kiss," said Aunt Lyda.

She had a pungent smell, not like her Grandma Johnson's talcum smell. Aunt Lyda did wear the same sort of dress that she remembered her Grandma wearing—flowery rayon with a big brooch holding the V-neck together and a narrow belt almost covered by her bosom. She carried a large white handbag over her arm. "Carry this for me, Annie," she said, handing the purse to Annie. "You've grown taller, haven't you?" The boys ran up the stairs ahead of her. Aunt Lyda had a hard time getting up, puffing loudly all the way.

The visit was a stiff one. They sat in the perfectly cleaned living room, holding cups of tea. Daddy was at work. Grandma Johnson's piano stood against one wall. "Play for us, Bonnie," Mama said.

Bonnie froze. "Please, Mother, not now. I haven't anything ready. I'm in the middle of a new piece."

"Play something, please," Mama insisted. But Bonnie refused and Mama finally let the subject drop. Bonnie could read the disappointment in her face.

"How are you, Aunt?" Mama asked.

"My heart is not good," Aunt Lyda replied with a sigh.

In her last letter, Grandma Johnson wrote that Lemmy and Violet were living with Lyda now that her husband had passed away. They had the upstairs bedroom, while Lyda slept on the enclosed front porch on a daybed. "Violet steals everything she can lay her hands on," she complained. Lemmy remained silent, never saying a word during the visit except once asking where the bathroom was.

Bonnie thought of her occasional pilfering ways and didn't blame Violet one bit. Life must have been hard for her, living next to Grandma Johnson, who had never approved of Lemmy's marriage to an Italian. Bonnie resisted her own stealing habit now, realizing that the trinkets she took became meaningless once she had them. *When I'm rich the awful temptation will be gone*, she thought. *I'll be accepted as being as good as the people who live on the east and west side of town. Is that why I've stolen? Committed a sin? Because I'm not accepted by them?*

The company didn't stay long, saying they were on their way south to visit Lyda's daughter Evelyn, who had married and moved to Green Bay. Bonnie recalled liking Evelyn, who was a pretty girl, older than Bonnie, always smiling and soft-spoken. That was on Fitch Street, in Negaunee where all the houses were the same. Company houses.

As the visitors stood to leave, Aunt Lyda took a wax-paper wrapped loaf of saffron bread from her large purse.

"Your mother made this for you, Helen" she said.

"Thank you, Aunt. Say thank you to my mother for me. I hope she's well."

"Her hearts not good either, Helen. You might try to visit her," said Aunt Lyda.

Bonnie saw her mother's crestfallen look at this veiled accusation. She knew there wasn't money for a trip. Mama had to keep her job at the restaurant to make ends meet since the glider plant closed. Daddy didn't make as much money as before, now that he worked at the wood lamp-making factory, and the playing gigs had fallen of, too.

When Daddy returned from the plant that evening, Mama told him about Bonnie's refusal to play. Daddy was angry, but now Bonnie was too big to spank. She stood cowering in front room as she listened to her parents argue.

"I'm tired, Helen. I work day and night and don't want to hear your complaints when I get home," yelled Daddy.

But Mama went on, "The paint on the kitchen ceiling is dirty from the flies, Will. I was embarrassed."

Daddy blew his top. "Shit" was his favorite expletive. "I'm sick and tired of painting that ceiling. Do it yourself."

He went into their bedroom, pulled some things out of a drawer, and put them into a paper sack. He took his good suit from the small closet and stormed out.

He was gone for three days. When he returned he and Mama didn't speak; Bonnie became a go-between communicator.

"Tell your father it's time for supper,"

"Tell your mother I need a better crease in my trousers."

Stuff like that. It went on for another few days before there was a thaw. That's what marrying for love means, Bonnie thought. *I'll marry for money and maybe love. Money first. Alfeo, Alfeo, Alfeo. You're the one. I do love you.*

Chapter 39

Normally the Green Dots met every morning near Joanne's locker before classes began. Now things had changed, the shift was in force. Instead, they met at Bonnie's locker, hoping to hear news of the Strongs. Bonnie would let them have little tidbits, some of them not entirely true. "There are fresh roses, white ones, delivered every afternoon. I answer the door and thank the delivery boy, you know, the one I went to the last prom with, the one whose father owns Ceresoli's flower shop." Quickly, she'd then turn the conversation in another direction.

"Joanne, are you still dating the baseball player, what's his name, Vance? He's rooming on the north side isn't he? I saw him at Al's Juke Box last Friday night. He was dancing with Shelly almost every dance. He's such a good dancer." Bonnie was happy to see Joanne's discomfort. *She's not the one with the power any longer*, she thought.

Joanne was quiet, not her usual style. She just gave her little annoying pursed lip 'humm'.

"Alice, can I look at your history notebook? I haven't quite finished the assignment. I'm so busy with Mrs. Strong. She wants me to call her Rosalie."

She enjoyed their stunned looks. There was the customary trading of pages and quick copying before the first bell rang. Even some of the popular girls said hi as they passed by. *Thank you, Miss Helmer*, she thought again. *I'm in a river going against the current, not toward the falls.*

"Hi, Bonnie. There's a party Saturday night at my house," Corrine, one of the popular girls, interrupted Bonnie's thoughts. "I hope you can come." Corrine's house was on the west side. Mrs. Strong said Bonnie could keep the Buick over the weekend. Surprisingly, she wanted Bonnie to pick her up for the High Mass on Sunday. Mr. Strong and Alfeo were out of town at one of their foundries.

Bonnie was thrilled at having the car. Mrs. Strong had grown to trust her driving skills. Now she would have a classy car to drive to Corrine's. Bonnie parked the car that Friday afternoon on Margaret Street, in front of the Bruno's Ford sedan, but not before driving around the block a few times, even farther, past the corner tavern, past Crispigna's store, and past the meat market.

Her mother came down the steps to view the commotion, and Tolly's workers came out from the bakery. Della, came out from across the street and looked on from her porch, and Mrs. Tomasi came out and waved to her mother.

Alfeo wasn't at the party, being out of town and he probably wouldn't have come anyway. He spent most of his free time with Alan. Corrine's parents weren't home and there was plenty of beer. Bonnie stuck to Coca-Cola. The living room was crowded with the partygoers. There was a back bedroom that some couples went into, coming out later looking flushed. Being curious, Bonnie peeked into the bedroom once, but it was dark, so she wasn't able to see much, just some vague tussling movement from under a bed cover.

She stepped out into the front yard, followed by the star football player, Jupe.

"Wait up, Bonnie," he called drunkenly. He grabbed clumsily for her, backing her into a tree and tried to kiss her, but he didn't look so appealing away from the football field. Bonnie pushed him off. *Someone else can have him,* she thought. *He's a north sider.*

"Come on, Bonnie, don't be holding back," he begged, as if his star power gave him the right to have his way with her. "Not tonight, Jupe, I have a headache." She gave him her teasing smile while pulling away. She left the party early.

On Sunday morning, she drove up the C Street hill to the Strongs. Mrs. Strong was waiting for her at the front door, wearing an elegant black silk suit and a small hat with a veil covering her eyes. That Sunday would be the first time she would attend Mass since Jean's terrible accident.

Bonnie wore the sweater Rosalie had given her. At the church, they walked to the very front pew. Mrs. Strong knelt through the entire Mass, head bowed. Gus was one of the servers, looking handsome in his cassock. He was taller than the priest, taller than the other altar boy.

"That's my brother," she whispered to Mrs. Strong. Mrs. Strong gave a slight nod of approval at that news. Daddy was there, too. He was in the choir loft at the back of the church, where he directed the choir in the *Kyrie, Gloria, Credo, Sanctus, Benedictus,* and *Agnus Dei.*

"*Agnus Dei,* The Lamb of God," murmured Rosalie. "You're my lamb, Bonnie."

"That's my dad directing the choir, too," Bonnie added. Mrs. Strong gave a little smile at this news.

Mr. Strong didn't attend church—*like my own mother*—Bonnie thought. Her mother spent Sunday mornings preparing the noon meal—her delicious pork roast, baked beans with salt pork, and browned potatoes. It was their favorite Sunday dinner, and one of the few times her family all sat down together.

Mrs. Strong was curious about Bonnie's family. "Tell me about your father and mother," Rosalie asked Bonnie one afternoon. Bonnie did some quick thinking. She didn't believe Mrs. Strong knew that she lived, above a bakery in four rooms with five other people.

"My father is a smart man," she began. He always helps me with my math and science homework. You know I study with Sister Carol for my piano lessons, but my dad has helped me in so many ways, especially with the scales and chords; minor scales, too. He works at a woodworking plant. He's so good with his hands—golden hands, my mother says. He's a strict Catholic, and he sees to it that I go to Confession every Saturday. And he leads us in a family rosary every night after supper." She left out the part about praying for her mother so that she would start going to church, but she did mention that her dad directed the choir at church for no money.

"That's good to hear," Mrs. Strong said. "And your mother, is she musical, too?

"Oh yes," said Bonnie. "She loves to hear me practice." That was a little lie, because she was always yelling, "Bonnie get away from that piano."

"She had piano lessons as a child," Bonnie went on, "and she taught me an easy way of reading the left-hand part. She's a wonderful cook, and she can sew almost anything on the sewing machine, and she loves to play Bingo at the church." She didn't mention that the closest her mother ever got to being in a church was the basement. Bonnie didn't mention her job at the restaurant, either, or her smoking and drinking.

"I lived on the northside, too, you know, before I was married, on Caspian Street." Bonnie knew that street. That was where more substantial houses were, stucco, two stories, with nice front lawns.

"I met Mr. Strong in Crispigna's store one day. It was raining and he offered to drive me home." *Rain again, water, a good omen*, thought Bonnie. *It rained the first time I came to the Strong castle.*

"I liked him right away," said Mrs. Strong. "He's a kind and funny man. We dated for a year before he asked me to marry him. He's generous, too, giving me anything I wish for. But he's a suspicious man. Maybe because of having his foundries in different places. It's a big responsibility. Sometimes he's caught a few of the employees stealing, tools and things like that. Earl sleeps with his wallet under his pillow." She started to laugh when she revealed this quirk. Bonnie joined in the laughter.

A few times, Mr. Strong came home before Bonnie left the castle. He always came into the library or kitchen to find Rosalie. He would kiss her warmly and put his arms around her in a comforting way, nodding to Bonnie before he left to make one of his many telephone calls. Bonnie heard some of these calls. They would erupt in anger at times. "What the fuck's, going on?" he would yell, and things like that.

They love each other, Bonnie thought. *He's pudgy and plain looking and has that toothpick which he manages to get to one side when he kisses Rosalie, and Mrs. Strong is so beautiful, even with the now white hair. They married for love, but the money insured that the love would last.* That's how it would be for her and Alfeo. She felt such tenderness for Alfeo, she *loved* Alfeo with all of her being, even though they had never met properly. Well, he was rich.

Bonnie still anguished at times about the problem of her protruding ear. She felt self-conscious when she had to wear her hair pulled back into a pony tail like Paula and Joanne, when the girls' trio performed in their pink, off the shoulder pique matching dresses.

Looking through a family album with Mrs. Strong one afternoon— most of the pictures were of Jean— she noticed the same flaw in one of Jean's first grade pictures. The left ear was Bonnie's eruption, while Jean's was on the right side.

It's kind of cute, she thought, and wondered if Jean had been subject to the same two-year baby bonnet torture as she had seen on herself in one of her baby pictures being held by Grandpa Johnson. Flat-eared people are so boring, she decided, and she started to wear her hair pulled back every day.

Rosalie had insisted that Bonnie help herself to any of the clothes in Jean's closet. "I just can't give them away," she said. "You remind me so much of Jean. Please, please do me this for me." Bonnie was happy to do Rosalie this favor.

When Bonnie finally entered her senior year. Alfeo, who had graduated the year before, was working with Mr. Strong at the foundry, though he still managed to be with Alan when he wasn't at work.

"He's not going to college, his mother said. "His father doesn't want him to get any funny ideas. He found him reading one of the books your brother, Alan, lent him—by some French writer—Camus, I think it was." They were in the library when Mrs. Strong revealed this. Looking around the book shelves, that revelation made sense to Bonnie. The books were all titled with names like *Being in the Will of God,* and The *Confessions of Saint Augustine,* and *The Lives of the Saints.* "I do like Alan." Rosalie went on. "I'm glad they spend so much time together. Alfeo needs a good friend."

Bonnie rarely saw Alfeo. Usually she was gone from the castle before he came home. When he did show up, he would greet his mother with a kiss on the cheek and nod briefly to Bonnie, almost as if she weren't there.

Bonnie refused to be discouraged. Hadn't her world shifted? Wasn't she in the castle? Wasn't she driving Rosalie's Buick? Mrs. Strong had begun to look a little happier. Sometimes she laughed with a soft chuckle when Bonnie read to her from the school newspaper.

Bonnie was now the editor of the paper, and even the year book, thanks to Mrs. Matthewson, the senior class advisor and English teacher. She had taken Bonnie under her wing when she learned of Bonnie's interest in Spanish and Latin.

Bonnie was in her third year of Latin and was learning the differences in pronunciation between classical Latin and church Latin. She was good at spelling and grammar, and went carefully over the articles submitted by the students for publication, taking care even with the corny jokes and sport news.

The Green Dots were impressed, even Mary Kay, who was the smartest one. They still talked about who they would marry and what sort of jobs they would get after graduation. Mary Kay was accepted at Michigan State; Shirley was going to nursing school at the University of Michigan. Alice said she would get married right away, after graduation, to Stephen, a college man. This surprised them all.

"He's Lutheran, like me," Alice explained. My parents think this is a good plan." *Her grades weren't that good*, Bonnie thought, *and Alice was probably glad that she didn't have to go to college, although she would leave Copper Ridge after the wedding.* "Stephen has a good job offer with a chemical company down state. Dow Chemical," she crowed. "He's graduating as a chemical engineer from Houghton Tech."

All the Green Dots were invited to the wedding at the Eastside Lutheran Church.

"You're not going, are you, Bonnie?" asked Sister Carol. "Have you talked to your father about this?"

Of course, she hadn't. Nor had she told her father about the time she'd played for Alice at the Order of the Eastern Star. "I'm going to the wedding, Mama," Bonnie said.

Mama said she didn't see anything wrong with it, but maybe Bonnie shouldn't say any of the prayers in case her father found out about it. "He's furious enough about your brother, Alan."

The wedding was a quiet affair. Bonnie wore one of Jean's organdy dresses, the same one she had worn to the Senior Girl's Tea. It was pretty and stuck out just so with the crinoline underneath, but it wrinkled quickly. Organdy was like that. Bonnie usually stood so the creases wouldn't be too noticeable. The fabric was hot, too, as was the church. After the short ceremony, everyone went to the church basement and had little cakes and some sort of fruit punch ladled from a cut-glass bowl, like the one at the country club, she noticed, but not as sparkly. This wasn't the sort of wedding Bonnie imagined for herself and Alfeo.

Chapter 40

By this time, Joanne was going steady with Vance, but she confided to Bonnie that she still hoped to connect with Alfeo. This was news to Bonnie.

"I know you went to prom with him last year, and you were in the play together. Have you kept in touch?" she asked.

"Not for a while, but I know he likes me," Joanne confided. "He's not been dating anyone since his sister's death. I don't suppose you run into him at the Strongs. Do you, humm?"

"I see him on occasion. He's busy with his dad," was all that Bonnie offered. Her head spun. What was Joanne thinking? Her twin, short-skirted banner waving, cheerleading cousins had graduated the year before, and the popular crowd was giving Joanne the cold shoulder as they were warming up to Bonnie. *Doesn't Joanne feel the shift?* She even felt a little sorry for Joanne. After all, life had thrown them together since the fifth grade—the walks to school, the girls' trio, the long telephone calls, the Girl Scouts, the forbidden comic books, and the Sunday afternoon movies.

Once they had even tried horseback riding together. It was a reward for selling the most Girl Scout cookies. They had been tied in sales, thanks to her own mother's patrons at the Italian restaurant. Joanne's mother was the troop leader, and of course, Joanne had the most medals.

Bonnie's bottom was sore for a week after that ride. She'd worried that her cherry, that—mysterious cherry—had been damaged, but no spot of blood appeared. Alfeo would be her first. Joanne was not in this picture. Bonnie would not share Alfeo.

The graduation ceremony went by in a blur. It was in the school auditorium. Her name was listed in the program. Bonnie Grace Smith; there was a little asterisk after her name. She was one of the top ten students—not in the National Honor Society, not going to college—and there was Joanne's name, no asterisk, but listed as a member of the Honor Society.

Bonnie's mother and father didn't attend. Daddy was playing a gig with Sammy and Frank, and Mama was working at Della's restaurant. Annie, Gus, and Alan, came, though, and so did Mrs. Strong. Bonnie saw her sitting to the side in the front row.

Mr. Strong was sitting on the stage with all the dignitaries. He was an important school board member. He didn't wear the ball cap or have the tooth pick between his teeth that night. He was one of the diploma presenters along with the superintendent of schools, and he nodded to Bonnie as he shook her hand.

Bonnie's feet, in the too-small high heeled white shoes with rounded toes, hurt so much that she almost tripped walking across the stage. The only shoe store still didn't carry her size. *Good old size nines again*, she thought. *I need at least a ten*. Rosalie smiled at her as she came back down the stage steps. Bonnie looked for her after the ceremony, but she had already left, *probably with Mr. Strong*, she thought. Mr. Strong drove a Buick, too.

Now that she had graduated, Bonnie, disappointed that she would not be going to college, applied for a job at the Bell Telephone Company. The head supervisor— an old maid, Miss Windale—said she would take her on. Miss Windale had spent all her working life with the company. Once she invited the telephone girls to her home for a little get together. "I own this house," she bragged. True, it was on the west side, but not the best part. All her furniture was white. The chairs, carpets, tables. *She still a virgin*, Bonnie thought. The many windows well-lit the house. *Her halo*, thought Bonnie.

She had a white parakeet in a cage with newspaper on the bottom for the droppings. "Andy talks," she said, but he never cooperated while the girls were there, despite Miss Windale's cooings and chirpings.

Life seemed strange without the Green Dots. Sally, who Bonnie saw on occasion, had finally decided to try for pre-med and was accepted at Northwestern. Bonnie still visited Mrs. Strong on Saturdays, but never saw her in church after that one time. She was filled with ennui, living above the bakery, getting up early to catch the bus for downtown. But she had money in her pocket now. The pay was good.

Joanne decided to enroll in nursing school, like Shirley. "I'll be going to Michael Reese in Chicago, humm," she said importantly on their last phone call before Joanne left.

Finding time to get to the Strongs' was growing harder. Still, Bonnie held tightly to her dream, although sometimes felt it fall away, and away, and away, almost out of her grasp. She wanted to have Alfeo, but she never saw him. *Where was he?*

Daddy still used her as a singer at the Riverside Club in Sammy's band on weekends. It seemed like another world, miles away from the telephone company. Sometimes she had a drink with alcohol; rum and Coke was her favorite. She was of age—eighteen— since during the war the drinking age had been lowered from twenty-one to eighteen for the soldier boys.

One Friday night, while she was singing "Kiss Me Once, and Kiss Me Twice, and Kiss Me Once Again" dressed in her favorite off-the-shoulder dark blue, sateen dress, and wearing black open-toed wedgie high heels with a strap back, and a silver buckle ornament clipped to the front, she saw them come in.

Mr. Strong and Alfeo, along with some other men she didn't recognize. *Now,* she thought, *this is the moment.* She began to move her hips a little as she sang and started to gesture with her arms. Usually she stood immobile as she sang. Her hair was pulled back. Her protruding ear wore a rhinestone clip-on earring with its twin on the other ear.

Mr. Strong and the other men were discussing business, she supposed, but Mr. Strong did glance her way. He said something to Alfeo, who shook his head no, but Mr. Strong kept at him, almost pushing him out of his chair. Alfeo looked at Bonnie as though he had never seen her before and was now seeing her for the first time. After her song, he came up to the bandstand and asked her to dance. *Just like*

Mama and Daddy, she thought, *only now there's money*. The next set was slow dances, and Bonnie and Alfeo danced them all.

There will be a wedding, a big one, she imagined. *She would borrow Aunt Lillian's wedding dress and veil, and there would be a choir of monks, and Sister Carol would be there and the Green Dots would be her attendants. Joanne would be the maid of honor and would arrange her bridal train and hold her flowers while Alfeo put the wedding ring on her finger, next to a two-caret diamond engagement ring.* She was in ecstasy as Alfeo steered her around the dance floor. Her feet no longer touched the ground.

Chapter 41

The following Monday, Bonnie worked the three-to-eleven shift at the telephone switchboard. She looked with envy at the glittering diamond on the hand of the girl at the next board. It was Corrine.

"Nice ring, Corrine," she said during a lull in number pleases. "When did you get it?"

"Dan proposed on Saturday, said Corrine. "We were at the J & R bar and he picked me up, sat me on the bar and said "Hey, Babe, let's get married."

"I said, 'yes', what else could I do? Right in front of everyone like that. They all cheered. Dan's a good guy. He works with his father at the flower shop. My folks like him, too. We're planning a Christmas wedding. Red velvet. I've always wanted a red-velvet wedding. I'll wear white, of course. My bridesmaids will be in the red. I'm so excited."

"That's great, Corrine," Bonnie said feeling a little envious. The switch board suddenly lit up and Bonnie proceeded in her usual quick manner of pulling up the cords from the metal base and plugging them into the small lights. There were five thousand lights to be answered.

"Number please? Thank you" Her nimble fingers flew like lightning, lifting the thick cords, plugging them in and pulling them out of the small holes as they blinked on and off. A surge of calls usually happened when there was a fire or an accident resulting in death. Bits of juicy gossip also resulted in calls back and forth. Operators weren't supposed to listen in on the conversations but Bonnie did when Miss Windale was on the far side of the room.

Copper Ridge was a noisy town. There were new babies, broken romances and cheating wives and husbands. Once she heard a conversation between Sally's dad and Adela Crispigna. They were arranging a rendezvous. That shocked Bonnie. Mrs. Crispigna was a stalwart in the Holy Martyrs altar society.

After nine o'clock the switchboard slowed down which gave her time to go over what had happened at the Riverside Club; the slow dances with Alfeo. *Was it a dream*, she wondered? It was only that one set, then she had to go back to the bandstand and sing the next number. When she finished, she had looked toward the Strong table but they had left.

A light came on in the upper corner in the 100 group of numbers. "Number please?" she said, breaking out of her daydream.

"Hey, Bonnie, it's Alfeo."

She recognized his voice immediately.

"We're not supposed to take personal calls while we're on shift," she whispered. She felt a lump in her throat. A warm shiver ran up and down her spine.

"I know," said Alfeo. "This is the first chance I've had to call since Friday night." He spoke quickly. "Can you come to my house for dinner next Friday before you go to the club? My mother's having a few relatives in from out of town. She wants them to meet you. You've been an angel for her since my sister died."

Bonnie was thrilled at the invitation. "Sure, Alfeo, but I'll need a ride to the Riverside after dinner. My dad leaves earlier with Sammy."

"Don't worry, Bonnie. I know where you live. I'll chauffer you around that evening," he said.

Bonnie agreed. *Is this a date*? she wondered. *Was this something arranged by Rosalie*? No matter, she would think of it as a date. It was in the stars.

The next day she told her mother about the invitation and the sort-of-date with Alfeo. Her mother looked alarmed.

"He's coming here? Your father must get at the kitchen ceiling. The flies have been thick this summer. The flypaper should come down."

"For god's sake Mama, forget the damn ceiling," Bonnie cried.

"He's not going to look at the ceiling. He works in a dirty foundry all day. I've seen him looking grimy."

"Well, it has to be cleaned," Mama insisted, "if I must do it myself, Bonnie Grace Smith."

That Friday, Bonnie dressed in one of Jean's dresses. The dress was a light rose color, sleeveless, with narrow shoulder straps. A deeper rose sash encircled her narrow waist. The evening was warm. She carried an off-white shrug and matching gloves for later that could be stuffed into her black satin handbag. She felt nervous. She had never been to dinner at the Strong castle.

She heard Alfeo on the steps. He knocked on the wooden wall all the way up the stairs. Her mother let him in the screen door.

"Hello, Mrs. Smith," he said, taking her hand. I'm here to chauffer Bonnie."

Bonnie was hiding in the front room, afraid of appearing too eager. She could hear her mother being fluttery, asking Alfeo if she could offer him something to drink.

"Oh, don't bother, Mrs. Smith. I see the refrigerator. I'll help myself." He walked over and opened the door, looked in and found a small bowl of left-over spaghetti. "That looks good," he said.

"Have some, please," said her mother.

"I'd better not. My mother's expecting Bonnie and me for dinner. Next time," he promised.

Bonnie liked his style, making himself right at home.

"Is Alan around?" he asked.

"He's at the library this evening, Alfeo," her mother said. "I'll tell him you were here."

Bonnie decided to put in her appearance, wobbling a little in her too small high heels. "Hi Alfeo," she said.

"Hi, Bonnie, ready?"

"Ready, Alfeo." She had never felt so ready.

"Be careful going down the stairs," her mother said.

"Don't worry, Mrs. Smith," said Alfeo with a smile, then took Bonnie's hand as he said goodbye.

The dinner was informal in a formal way. Mrs. Prianti was the chef and server. She stayed for the whole affair. She served the food in courses. Egg drop soup, risotto, tossed salad, roast veal, asparagus, and finally sliced pears with bleu cheese.

Bonnie had always thought bleu cheese tasted like soap, but she took a small piece. *I will learn to like this stuff*, she thought. She had eaten only a little of each course, not wanting a full stomach when she sang later at the Riverside.

Mr. Strong ate heartily, asking for seconds of everything. "Eat, eat," he told Bonnie.

Bonnie noticed he didn't have the toothpick in his mouth. She heard the guest, Mrs. Oliva, mention to Rosalie, "Bonnie looks so much like Jean."

There it was again. The resemblance thing. It was getting tiring. *I'm me*, Bonnie thought, *not Jean*. She watched as Mrs. Strong bowed her head momentarily and Mr. Strong put his hand briefly on her arm. It was only a moment, an uncomfortable lull in the conversation.

Mrs. Oliva looked embarrassed at her faux pas, but then all was right again and the light conversation about nothing continued.

"I have to get going, Alfeo," Bonnie said. "It's almost eight-thirty."

"Mother, we have to leave," said Alfeo, apologetically

"Yes, I know sweetheart, have a nice time," she said, with a look of approval. She looked happy that evening, her eyes glowing, her white hair beautifully arranged in a thick chignon, a diamond studded brooch fastened to the shoulder of her grey silk, long sleeved gown.

Someday, that's how I will be, thought Bonnie, *the queen of the castle*. She said her goodbyes and left holding on to Alfeo's arm. Alfeo followed through with his promise, getting her to the club, then home again. He walked her up the twenty-six steps and gave her a pecky kiss on the cheek as he said, "Goodnight, Bonnie."

That was all. Her mother was waiting up for her, wanting to know every detail from the evening. But Bonnie was tired.

"We'll talk tomorrow, Mama," she said. She wasn't sure herself what the evening meant. She had been striving hard toward her goal—Alfeo, and rich. Rich and Alfeo.

The next morning, she told Alan about seeing Alfeo. Alan didn't respond except to say, "That's nice, Bonnie." He and Alfeo were still close friends. They spent almost every Saturday and Sunday together at the golf course in summer and at a shooting range or pool parlor when the weather closed in. *He knows Alfeo better than I do*, thought Bonnie, *but that will change.* She knew she was in a winning game.

The next six months were a repetition of that first Friday night dinners at the Strongs'. *Well, at last I'm making the First Fridays,* she thought. *A different kind of First Fridays. A better kind.* She wished Alfeo would progress beyond the cheek peck, though. He seemed immune to her best shine.

Bonnie's mother adored Alfeo. She always had some tempting tidbit in the refrigerator for him to discover when he came for Bonnie. Knock, knock, knock on the wall as he came up the steps. He never once looked at the ceiling. He had begun to call Mama, Helen. Mama obviously loved it.

"It's always nice to see you, Alfeo. My, you look especially handsome tonight" she would say as he took her hand.

God, is she flirting? thought Bonnie.

Daddy only saw Alfeo at the club. Sometimes he came and sat with Alfeo and Bonnie during breaks. Not much was spoken beyond "How are you, Alfeo?"

"Can I get you something to drink, Mr. Smith?"

Father didn't drink. "You can buy me a ginger ale," he allowed. Then the owner will keep hiring us. They'll charge for a whiskey and soda, though. Alfeo didn't mind. "I understand," he said. "It's good for business."

Bonnie now liked scotch on the rocks. She limited herself to one and made it last all evening by adding little bits of water and ice to the glass as she sipped the stinging liquid.

In February, Alfeo asked Bonnie to marry him. It was on a blustery night. Her feet were freezing because the heater in his Buick wasn't working.

"My feet are cold," she said.

"Take you shoes off, I'll rub them warm."

As he massaged her feet, he said, "I want to marry you Bonnie."

The warmth from the foot-rubbing raced through her body. She said, "Oh, yes, yes, Alfeo"

He kept rubbing as he said, "My mother thinks we should be married in August, on the Feast of the Assumption That's six months from now. She wants time to plan."

"Plan what, Alfeo?" asked Bonnie. "It'll have to be a small ceremony. My family can't afford much. Why do we have to wait?"

"My dad will want his business associates there and my mother comes from a pretty big Italian family. She doesn't want to offend anyone. Dad will handle the expenses. Don't worry."

Bonnie thought, *well, let them pay. This is what I've been waiting for my whole life. They can pay. My parents will agree. I'll have a wonderful wedding. It's only right for my new life to come.*

"Tomorrow, we'll go to Fugeres Jewelry store and pick out a ring," he said. My dad will announce the engagement at next Friday night's dinner."

"I thought you were doing something with Alan tomorrow, Alfeo" she said. "He looks forward to seeing you. This is his last year in high school."

Bonnie had come to appreciate Alan's faithfulness to Alfeo. *They have something special,* she thought. *He'll be part of my new family.*

"Mother says we must have the ring by next Friday," said Alfeo insistently. "It won't take all day and I can still meet Alan at the pool hall."

Who am I marrying, Rosalie or Alfeo, thought Bonnie. *Oh, well, my feet are warm and I won't worry about things like a ring or whose paying for my wedding.*

Her mother was waiting again, sitting at the kitchen table with her glass of beer.

"I'm getting married, Mama," Bonnie said.

Her mother looked relieved. She came toward Bonnie and embraced her. "I'm glad, Bonnie," she said. Bonnie couldn't remember the last time her mother had touched her.

"Go to bed, Mama, before Daddy gets home," said Bonnie. "You must be tired, waiting all this time." Bonnie was exhausted, too. It had been a long quest. She would soon be leaving her familiar home. Her safe place. A loved place.

Chapter 42

On the eve of the wedding, a Friday, Bonnie and Alfeo arrived at the church before the others in the party who were coming for the wedding rehearsal. It was confession time. It was Bonnie's first confession in several weeks. She confessed her usual only venial sins and knelt for her penance—the customary three Hail Marys—then waited for Alfeo to come out of the curtained box. She wished she could hear his sins. *He's been in there quite a long time. What could be the mortal sin that was keeping him in there so long*? thought Bonnie. He had never tried to embrace her or give her more than a small peck on the cheek. She was sure that he had remained a virgin, too.

The day of the wedding, she dressed, with her mother's help, in the apartment above the bakery. She donned her Aunt Lillian's satin wedding dress. It fit perfectly. She had her mother's pretty engagement chain around her neck. Annie helped, too. She was in the wedding party, and wore a long lavender taffeta dress.

It was summer and the Green Dots were on break from school. Even Alice came from Lower Michigan to mark the occasion. They made up the rest of the bridal party and wore the same lavender ruffled gowns. Joanne's dressmaker made them, copied from a picture in a bridal magazine. Annie's dress was a bit to snug around her middle, and it was a struggle to get the zipper up. She had a forlorn look on her face.

"What's the problem, Annie?" asked Bonnie.

Annie didn't answer.

"Annie's going to live with Second Cousin Evelyn in Green Bay for her senior year, Bonnie. That will keep her away from the fast crowd for a while," Mama said.

Gus was going to be a server at the solemn high Mass. *I can't believe there will be three priests,* thought Bonnie. Gus hadn't arrived yet, but he told Daddy he would be on time, arriving with Mr. Gorman. Alan had said he wouldn't come to the church.

"Please come, Alan, just this once," Bonnie had pleaded with him that morning. "Alfeo is your good friend, your best friend."

"It won't be the same now, Bonnie. I do wish you the very best." He looked so sad. "It's hot today," he went on. It was August. "I think I'll go for a quick swim in Lake Wakesha."

"You don't need those heavy hiking boots for that," said Bonnie.

"I may go up the hill later for some blackberries. They're in season now." He gave Bonnie a hug and said to give Alfeo a hug from him.

At last she was ready. Her mother said, "You look beautiful, Bonnie Grace."

Bonnie walked carefully down the twenty-six steps, trying not to muss her gown. Annie carried her flowers, a bouquet of daisies and baby's breath. She and Annie got into the back seat of the Model A and headed for the Holy Martyr's Church.

Mama, dressed in the obligatory pink, sat in the front pew. At the church, Bonnie took Daddy's arm as he led her down the familiar aisle. Daddy's pants were carefully creased, but a little shiny from the frequent pressings. He had a daisy boutonniere in his best, band gig jacket. The Green Dots walked ahead in measured steps as the music began. Joanne bent to fix Bonnie's train before taking her place in line. Bonnie murmured her thanks while giving her a little smile of triumph.

She had given Joanne her scrapbook of saints and martyrs pictures as a bridal gift to the maid of honor. "Here, Joanne," she said as she gave her the beautifully wrapped book. "It's my dearest treasure. I've never told you sorry how I am that Vance took off with Shelly. Remember I wrote you about that?" You must have been heartbroken".

"I got over it, Bonnie. Traveling around with a baseball team was not the sort of life I'd imagined. I hear they're married and living in

Detroit, now," said Joanne wistfully, ending with her familiar self-satisfied humm. Bonnie suddenly found this mannerism endearing.

"Joanne, I've put Tom Jones' army base address under the front cover. Do you remember him? He's coming back to Copper Ridge in another six months. You should write to him. I'll bet he's lonely. He told me once that he thought you were quite a girl, sticking with the Girl Scouts for so long."

"Thanks, Bonnie. You've always been my best friend, humm"

"I'll be sure to throw my bouquet in your direction at the reception." Bonnie enjoyed feeling magnanimous. *Yes, we will always be friends*, she thought as she proceeded down the church aisle. She nodded to Sister Carol as she passed her, sitting ten rows back on the Strong side.

The music was beautiful. Mr. Strong had arranged for a monk's choir to come all the way from a monastery in Green Bay. Mrs. Strong, wearing mother-of-the groom blue, nodded to her with an approving look. Alfeo was waiting for her at the head of the aisle.

Bonnie felt a little lightheaded standing before the priests, who waved the censer with the holy incense about each other as if they were the ones being married. Her hand shook as Alfeo pushed the wedding band onto her nervous finger. The gold band matched a one-carat diamond engagement ring that she wore on her right hand during the ceremony. She would transfer it to her left hand and pair it with the wedding band after the ceremony. *This band will never come off,* Bonnie vowed inwardly.

The reception took place at an exclusive private club, all arranged and paid for by Mr. Strong. There was an open bar. The food was prepared by Mrs. Prianti. Little girls with long hair ribbons streaming down their backs carried small white baskets of confetti candy as they walked among the tables set outside on the green lawn. Rosalie whispered to Bonnie that she had arranged a honeymoon trip for the newlyweds to the shrine of St. Anne de Beaupre in Quebec. Bonnie's mother was overcome at the news and had to be helped to the ladies' room. The music was played by an Italian brass band, members of The Sons of Venice.

A black and white photo shows Bonnie in Aunt Lillian's white satin bridal gown. She is standing next to Alfeo and has her hand on his arm. She is wearing glasses. Alfeo is only slightly taller than Bonnie. Bonnie's veil covers her long wavy hair almost completely, like a nun's veil, except for the curved long bang covering her forehead. They are standing outside on the church lawn. The Green Dots flank the couple on either side. Everyone is looking straight ahead. No one is smiling. There is a priest, a Monsignor, standing behind the group, wearing a black biretta hat.

After the reception, Alfeo drove her to the bakery so she could change into her going away suit of cream faille. He went up the twenty-six steps with her.

"I want to say goodbye to Alan," he said. "He wasn't at the wedding."

"Alan said he was going swimming, Alfeo. I'll ask Mama if he's come back."

Her mother was in the bedroom, resting with a cold cloth on her head. Her false teeth were in a glass of water near the bed. "We're leaving, Mama. Alfeo wants to say goodbye to Alan"

"I don't know where he is," said Mama in a slurred, worried voice. "He hasn't come back from swimming."

"Well, tell him we said goodbye, okay, Mama? We've got to get on the road before it gets too late."

Mother made no answer.

In the car, sitting next to Alfeo, Bonnie felt nervous. *What should we talk about*, she wondered? She didn't have to wonder for long. Alfeo stopped on the way out of town at the local tobacco and magazine store.

"Wait here, Bonnie. I'll only be a minute," he apologized.

He returned to the car with several Classic Illustrated comic books. *Ivanhoe, The Woman in White, The Last of the Mohicans*, and *Tale of Two Cities*.

"It's a long drive to Quebec," he said. "Would you mind driving for a while? I'm a little tired. I'd like to catch up on reading these. Mother wants me to read more of the classics."

Comic books, thought Bonnie. *This is a peculiar start to a honeymoon.*

Alice had gone to Niagara Falls. Here I am going to a shrine at St. Anne de Beaupre.

"Sure Alfeo, I like to drive," said Bonnie. Other than the obligatory quick kiss in the church, Alfeo had made no effort to embrace her or even hold her hand. *He must be nervous, too*, she thought.

She drove along the entire route, following Lake Michigan on the southern side of the Upper Peninsula, using a map given to her by Mr. Strong. They stopped twice for gas and a sandwich along the way. Bonnie wasn't hungry. There had been so much food at the reception.

Alfeo read the comic books more than once. Sometimes he made a comment about a scene in the book as Bonnie drove. It had been an exhausting day. *These are not the kind of books he shares with Alan*, she thought. *Who is Alfeo, anyway? What have I bought into?*

"Can we stop soon?" asked Bonnie. "It's getting dark, and now it's starting to rain."

"As soon as we cross over to Canada, Bonnie. We're almost to Windsor."

Bonnie found the bed and breakfast without trouble. It was right along the Kings Highway.

The owner, Mrs. Fleury, greeted them with a knowing smile.

"I'm Mrs. Strong's second cousin," she said. I knew you were coming. Your room is upstairs. Sleep in if you want to. I'll hold breakfast for you." She led them up the stairs.

Alfeo carried their bags into a well-furnished room.

"The bathroom's down the hall to you right, dears," Mrs. Fleury said.

"This is a nice room, don't you think, Alfeo? Look at the pretty lamp. Is there a church nearby, Mrs. Fleury" Tomorrow is Sunday and we don't want to miss Mass, do we Alfeo?" *Am I crazy*, thought Bonnie? *This is the night. The night I finally give it up. My virginity. What am I babbling on about?*

"A church. Yes," said Mrs Fleury. It's about a kilometer east, right along this highway. They have a late service. Now, you two get some rest. I know you've come a long way. Alfeo, I talked to your mother early this morning on the telephone, by long distance. She wanted to be sure you made it here."

Bonnie knew all about long distance. She'd put through many of those calls during her time at Bell Telephone. She'd said her goodbyes to everyone there. Alfeo said he didn't want her to work. She'd have her hands full, running the household with his mother. *Ah, Rosalie. Her long distance was only as far as a phone call,* Bonnie thought.

After Mrs. Fleury left, the newlyweds stood awkwardly, unable to make eye contact.

"Well, let's get on with it Bonnie. You're my wife now. Are you happy?"

"Oh yes, Alfeo. I'm so happy. I've loved you for so long." She started to shiver. Alfeo gave her an odd look.

Bonnie opened her small suitcase and began to take off her going-away suit. She had purchased a white, lacy, sheer nightgown and matching peignoir. She held it up in front of her to show Alfeo.

"That's pretty, Bonnie, but there's no need to put it on." By this time Alfeo had removed his clothes and he shyly embraced Bonnie as he led her to the bed. His smooth hairless skin felt pleasantly cool to Bonnie.

"I'm inexperienced, Alfeo," said Bonnie hesitantly.

"As am I, Bonnie, but I have a good idea of the procedure."

The procedure was over in short order, and Bonnie gave a little cry as Alfeo entered her. Alfeo turned his back to her afterwards and fell immediately asleep. He hadn't kissed her.

Bonnie didn't sleep. *I've reached my goal,* she thought. *Now what?* She began to plan the next step. *Mama and Daddy should have a better place to live. I'll ask Alfeo to get them a house on Caspian Street, near Rosalie's parents, the Nanninis. Won't the neighbors be surprised? Daddy will be closer to Holy Martyr's Church, and Mama won't have to climb steps with the laundry basket. I can drive her to Negaunee to visit her mother and father. Maybe Mr. Strong will give Daddy a good job at his foundry—an office job. Daddy is so smart.*

As soon as it was light, she examined the bed sheet. There it was, the red spot. *People make so much about this spot,* she thought. *It's nothing, really. A quick stab and being a virgin is no more.* She cuddled up to Alfeo and finally fell into a deep sleep.

The sun was high in the sky when she woke and realized Alfeo's skin was burning hot. She shook him awake.

"I think you're sick Alfeo," she said.

Alfeo moaned and said something incoherent. Bonnie called down to Mrs. Fleury.

"I need a doctor, my husband's ill." It was the first time she had said "my husband." It seemed strange.

"I've seen this happen to virgin honeymooners a few times before," said the local doctor. I believe he's having a reaction to your vaginal fluid. Yes. Keep cool cloths on his wrists and forehead. He'll survive. Don't worry, Missus, it only happens the one time."

They stayed another night at the bed and breakfast. Bonnie anxiously tended to the wet, cold cloths until Alfeo's fever subsided. She remembered Cousin Jackie, who had to be packed in ice for twenty-four hours. She hoped Alfeo would not become an insatiable eater like her cousin. Bonnie didn't want to drive a disguised hearse.

"I feel awful," said Alfeo.

"The doctor said you'll be better soon, Alfeo. I was worried about you. Try to get a little more rest, Honey." *Had she called him Honey?* It seemed to fall from her lips so naturally.

There was a knock on the bedroom door and Mrs. Fleury looked in.

"Alfeo's mother called," said Mrs. Fleury. "She wants you to come straight home."

"We'll be on our way soon," said Bonnie irritably, thinking Rosalie might become an enemy rather than a friend. She certainly was keeping track of them. Her own mother kept out of Bonnie's business to a fault.

"You'll have to drive again, Bonnie," said Alfeo. "I'm glad you're such a good driver."

On the drive to Copper Ridge, they stopped almost every hour so that a moaning Alfeo could get out of the car and throw up. He left the Classic Illustrated comics on the back seat.

So, this is how my new rich life begins, thought Bonnie. *No Niagara Falls, no miracle at St. Anne de Beaupre, and a sick husband.*

"I'm terribly sorry, Bonnie," said Alfeo, weakly, seeming to sense Bonnie's disappointment.

"That's okay, Alfeo. They only speak French in Quebec. We wouldn't have understood a word. I only know Latin and Spanish." Bonnie started to laugh, and laughed so hard she began to cry. Her tears made it hard to see the road. It was raining full force now. *In a few months, the snow will begin,* she thought. *Cold. I like the cold.*

Her vagina—which had made her new husband sick—still felt sore. There would have to be some better instruction in what Alfeo had called "the procedure." She'd read that lovemaking was a pleasurable act. *I hope he's trainable.* She continued to laugh to herself at the thought.

Alfeo threw up one last time. "I feel better now, Bonnie," he said, while reaching for the Classic Comics in the back seat of the car. They drove in silence for the rest of the way to Copper Ridge.

I'm leaving my safe place, the bakery, it was a hard place, but a safe place—the four rooms, the hiding places, Mama, Daddy, the bakery smells, the twenty-six steps, Margaret Street, Crispigna's store, everything familiar. I've reached my goal, but I'm a little scared. Bonnie's thoughts continued to skitter as she drove.

The rain had let up when they arrived at the castle on C Street in Copper Ridge. Bonnie saw Rosalie waiting expectantly at the front door. She ran towards them as they got out of the car and threw her arms around them in a possessive embrace.

"Welcome home, children," she cried.

End

CPSIA information can be obtained
at www.ICGtesting.com
Printed in the USA
BVOW06*1821080218
507653BV00002B/3/P